IN MY OTHER LIFE

Publication of this book was supported by a grant from
the National Endowment for the Arts.

Also by Joan Silber

Household Words

In the City

In My Other Life

STORIES

Joan Silber

Sarabande Books
LOUISVILLE, KENTUCKY

FIRST EDITION

Managing Editor
Sarabande Books, Inc.
2234 Dundee Road, Suite 200
Louisville, KY 40205

LIBRARY OF CONGRESS CATALOGING-IN-PUBLICATION DATA

Silber, Joan.
In my other life : stories / by Joan Silber.
p. cm.
ISBN 1-889330-42-6 (cloth : alk. paper). — ISBN 1-889330-43-4 (pbk : alk. paper)
I. Title.
PS3569.I414I48 2000
813'.54—DC21 99-37966
CIP

Cover: *Manhattan 4*, by Ron Milewicz. Used by kind permission of the artist.

Cover and text design by Charles Casey Martin.

Manufactured in the United States of America.
This book is printed on acid-free paper.

Sarabande Books is a nonprofit literary organization.

For my friend Lynn Myers
1947–1989

ACKNOWLEDGMENTS

These stories appeared previously in the following publications: "Bobby Jackson" in *Witness*, "Lake Natasink" in *The New Yorker*, "Without Ellie" and "What Lasts" in *Boulevard*, "Ragazzi" in *Michigan Quarterly Review*, "Partners" in *The Voice Literary Supplement*, "The Dollar in Italy" in *Global City Review*, "Ordinary" in the *Chicago Tribune*, "First Marriage" in *River City*, "Commendable" in *Ploughshares*, and a section from "Comforts" in *The Binnewater Tides*. "The Dollar in Italy" is included in *An Inn Near Kyoto: Writing by American Women Abroad* [New Rivers Press, 1999].

I would like to thank the Djerassi Foundation, the Millay Colony, the Virginia Center for the Creative Arts, and the MacDowell Colony for support during the writing of these stories.

CONTENTS

Bobby Jackson

We were sitting around at night after work. I was a busboy at the time, hanging around in my sweaty T-shirt, drinking free Jack Daniel's. The bar didn't close until four in the morning, but the staff got off anywhere from eleven on and gathered at one of the booths. Nancy, my favorite of the waitresses, was braiding my ponytail and fidgeting with my sideburns and arguing with me. Nancy was waiting for her boyfriend, an English guy who was a painter. I used to torment her by singing, "England swings, like a pendulum do." She liked me well enough to flirt, and during work hours we would stand near the bus-box with our arms around each other's waists, very friendly and collegial.

"Totally wrong," Nancy said. We were arguing about the restaurant's cats. Gordon, the owner, had brought in a cat to fend off the rats in the basement. The cat was a scared, undersized adolescent who had surprised everyone by having a litter of kittens right away.

Did people mind if the kittens were all over the place, climbing on tables, stepping into dinner plates? I said yes, Nancy said no. Nancy's friend Donna said, "Find one person sober enough to notice."

I got up and walked through the aisles looking. This was in 1969 and I was twenty-two, showing off. I ran into Bobby Jackson, the second cook, coming out of the men's room after his shift, and I brought him to the table as my specimen of sobriety. Bobby grouched about the cats, but he was the one who fed them shrimp scraps. Every night he whispered to them on the cellar stairs, *psst*, chow time. When he shut the door fast, he'd seen a rat.

By the time we got to the table, Nancy was off cats and on the subject of where she was saving money to travel to. Even as a busboy I was doing pretty well financially. The restaurant was a madhouse. Every night it got more packed and noisy and out of control; it was having its day as the red-hot center. My own plan was to go to India. "Step outside for free," Bobby Jackson said. "We got Bombay right here." Aziz, the porter, had taught me some words in Urdu, which I made everyone listen to. He had drilled me in dirty slang, long insults about your grandmother's private parts. "Get in trouble that way," Bobby Jackson said. "Come back as a chutney yourself."

At first we'd all thought Bobby Jackson was from the South. He spoke in a slow drawl, he walked with a stoop. Nancy used to imitate his way of looking at us sideways like Stepin Fetchit. When she showed Bobby, he did one of his low snorty chuckles. Nancy was from Virginia; I thought she understood Bobby better than I did, to know what he'd take as a joke.

Actually Bobby was from Harlem. And he was a lot younger than he looked; he was twenty-five. After his shift he had a long subway ride home. If he fell asleep on the train, he woke up going the wrong way back downtown. Sometimes he fell asleep again and wound up on the subway all night. He would talk about it the next day, shaking his head and snorting at himself.

I think we were his first downtown job. God knows we thought we were interesting. At the moment Nancy and Donna were putting Led Zeppelin on the jukebox, which Gordon the owner was famous for hating. They had a bet going about how many seconds it would take Gordon to turn it off. Bobby was into this, and he raised the bet by a quarter. I was in such a good mood I didn't even mind that much when Nancy's boyfriend showed up. I made room for him at the table, and I stayed around after they left.

I WAS NEVER A GREAT BUSBOY. I sort of worked my tail off in fits and starts and then malingered in between. I had been like that in college too. All the same, when one of the bartenders was fired for stealing, I got promoted to working behind the bar. "Climbing that corporate ladder," Bobby Jackson said. I had to train, which meant learning to make five basic drinks and listening while Gordon told me he had one piece of advice. Actually he had several. "This is it," he said. "You can drink it, you can give it away, you can steal it, but you can't do all three."

Bobby Jackson was at the bar at the time getting himself a belt of ginger ale, and he gave me a fish-eyed, knowing look. "Huh, our Gordon," he said to me later. "Malcolm Forbes."

Bobby himself had started as the dishwasher. It was Reginald the chef's idea to train him for greater things. Bobby's cooking (cold appetizers and grilled items) was fine but he was slow—that was his one big drawback—and he was accident-prone. He cut his hand all the time opening the clams and oysters; he seemed to forget his own palm was under the shell. He'd come to the bar looking like a train wreck, and I'd put vodka on the bleeding cut. I'd pour him a shot of

Dewar's—his brand, but he'd swallow it in one shudder and make a face. Usually he said, "That scotch is nasty stuff."

I was doing better with women since I'd been made a bartender. Women would hang around till my shift was over. Beautiful, hip women, some of them; I had my flings. Brief flings, but usually good-willed on both sides. Nancy went around insulting me, which I took as a sign of interest. She'd complain about my sloppy martinis when she came to pick up her drinks. Once she pelted my T-shirt with maraschino cherries, very fifth-grade.

We were all keyed up from working at full tilt. The pace of customers kept us going, and the jukebox. Nancy walked around singing lyrics to herself and being rude to people at her tables. She'd tell them the fish of the day was tadpole; she'd walk away if they took too long ordering. Bobby liked Nancy. He called her Miss Nan.

I was waiting out Nancy's romance with the Brit. I liked to watch her parading around the floor in her micro-miniskirt and her black taffeta apron, like a French maid's. As far as I could see, a good part of her life was spent dealing with men expressing their lust in various ways. Mostly it wasn't any kind of aggravation to her. She brightened, out on the floor. All this brightness helped me.

One night Nancy came down into the basement after I had been tapping a beer keg, and there was no one else there. I moved in for the clinch and there we were, finally, a kissing couple. For the rest of the night I could hardly stand it. But when we both got off work, we hung around drinking at one of the booths. I don't know why we did this, although I remember that hour at the end of the night as festive and sexy.

Bobby sat with us, and a lot of other people settled in. Nancy was talking about where her family lived in Virginia, and Bobby wanted to know if they had horses. It turned out Bobby was crazy about horses. Who would have guessed this? Nancy said her family had horses when she was little, but then her father's business slipped and he had to sell them. "Should've sold the children and kept the horses," Bobby said.

Bobby told us he'd gone riding a bunch of times from the stables near Central Park. Had I ever been there? I hadn't.

"My father keeps driving his company into the ground but he always bounces back," Nancy said.

"Probably has something to bounce on," Bobby said. "Money."

There was a discussion about what you would do if you lost everything—none of us had anything, but in any case no one could picture not being able to start over. You could sell stuff in the street, you could go back to school, you could always hustle somehow. Donna and Marcia, another waitress, talked about how much you could actually make being a hooker. Hector, one of the customers, talked about karma and dealing with the task given to you. We were a strange mix of the spoiled and the soupy and the game.

Jay the bartender went into a story about losing money at the track and by the time he finished it, Bobby Jackson was asleep with his head on the table and Nancy was giving me the eye. Jay said he would get Bobby up later and make sure he got on the subway. I certainly didn't want to be the one to do it then.

But in fact Nancy and I went off to another bar, a darker, louder one than ours. Why did we have to do this? We were aching to get into bed, but all we could think of was more parading around, more social excitement. We believed the real world was in the public life of the night, and we wanted one more dip while we were feeling good.

WE DID GET HOME TO MY PLACE finally, and after that night I was a man drowned in love, or at least paralytic lust. All I did in my waking hours was have erotic daydreams about Nancy, or else I really was with Nancy. I was swimming around in fulfilled wishes. I thought this was because I had attained whatever knowledge it takes to be lucky.

The whole first month we didn't get out of bed till three in the afternoon. It wasn't only the sex that kept us there, but those afternoon sleeps, the waves of waking and sliding back—the ghostly freedom and the delicious waste. Sometimes we were still in bed at twilight, when squares of blue light showed at the windows.

We had fights, of course. Nancy was a moody and demanding person, and she could turn on me when I least expected it. Also I got sidetracked myself; I forgot when I was supposed to meet her places. Mostly we didn't go anywhere much; we moved around from our bar to the other bar people went to, in a loop.

It was around this time that Bobby asked Nancy to get him some acid. He didn't like it, as it turned out. "Could forget where you parked your mind, on that," he said. He had taken it after work, in his leisure time. But what was he doing standing around in his apron at two in the morning, tripping, in the middle of a room filled with milling white strangers? He must have been as curious as anyone, as eager to see what he could in his time around us.

One night when Nancy and I both got off work early, we told Bobby to meet us at the other bar. The place had a disco upstairs, and in the crowd we forgot about Bobby when he didn't come. The next day Bobby told Nancy he'd shown up but they hadn't let him in. All full tonight, the bouncer said. They let in blacks but not blacks who looked like Bobby, with his stingy-brim hat and his banlon shirt. "Shit," Nancy said, "we should've known." "I'm a jerk," I said to Bobby. Bobby just rolled his eyes to the side. None of us wanted to talk about it.

Probably Bobby had wanted to see the other bar, which was

bigger and more famous than ours, although not famous in his circles. We didn't ask too much about his circles. Jay knew more than we did. Jay went uptown with him to buy drugs.

It was from Jay that I first heard that Bobby was a junkie. Jay said, "You knew, right?" Maybe I half-knew. Actually I don't think so. And once we all knew, I thought there must be thousands of people like Bobby, holding down jobs, showing up every day, doing what they had to, for years and years. Even Gordon didn't care really. Bobby was slow, but not crazy or raging or alcoholic, like half the kitchen staff .

Jay asked if I was by any chance interested in going uptown with them the next time. Jay was out to extend my education. Nancy was not pleased about my going on this buying trip. "One short ride on the subway," I said.

We went after midnight, and the subway car, with its few solemn riders, emptied out, stop by stop, until there was just us and a cluster of black and Hispanic people wondering if Jay and I knew where the hell we were going. I said something to Jay about how if we had to travel this long to get high we must be truly dedicated. "Sincere is the word," Bobby said. I said, "High-minded." Jay groaned, and Bobby did his long hissing laugh. He jabbed my shoulder, an unusual sign of giddiness from him. Three jolly guys, that was us.

125th Street was hopping when we got out—a summer night, everybody on the street, radios going full blast. Nobody acted as if we were worth noticing. We cruised along with Bobby for a few blocks and he was quiet, with the same stillness in his face he had at work. Jay and I managed to shut up, but we were nosy and tense and exhilarated. At a corner a man came up to Bobby and clapped him on the back, very chummy. "What do you know?" Bobby said. "Hey."

Upstairs in someone's apartment, Bobby was all business. No winks or nods, no horsing around, no chatty introductions. Contrary to what you hear now, nobody wanted us to shoot up right then and there to prove we weren't undercover somebodies; they wanted us to pay and get out. In the kitchen, where they took us, there was only the dealer and a very skinny girl sitting on the floor drinking a beer. We shook hands all around, and the guy made a salesman's sort of joke about our long journey to get the best. The dealer was not young, and he was loud-voiced and hearty, like somebody's uncle. I could hear men's voices in another room and a TV tuned to a program with a laugh track. "How long did it take you to grow that ponytail?" the dealer said to me. "Couple years, man," I said. "Very stylish," he said. "All my friends are stylish," Bobby said. "Do tell," the dealer said.

Bobby went with us back down to the street, like a man walking his date to a cab. I was disappointed that things had happened so quickly—I felt overprotected, the way women must feel in the face of certain gallantries. Bobby, who'd made a purchase himself, must've been eager to get home, but he lingered with us on the block. He talked for a few minutes about how the night had cooled off. Not an interesting subject, and none of us were what you could call relaxed, but we made some jokes about the air conditioner at work and how cheap Gordon was, and we hovered around aimlessly, as if we were high already. Bobby was in good spirits when we said good night.

As it turned out, that was my one trip up there. Bobby didn't take us again, not me anyway. Still, the next day, Bobby said, "Everything okay? Glad to hear it. Everything fine, right?" He must've been glad enough to show off for us. In our various ways, we were all three proud of our teamwork. "Hands across the waters," Jay said. Jay was especially thrilled with what we'd brought back—you'd think he'd smuggled it from the poppy fields personally—and it was in fact stronger than any heroin I'd had, not that I'd had so much. I'd had some.

Nancy was not overjoyed about any of this, although I couldn't keep from bragging to her anyway. It was a big topic between us from then on. We had a scene about it right in the middle of work, during a slow spell. For a Southern girl, Nancy had a voice that could get very shrill, and I couldn't, of course, be argued out of anything. She warned me about all the parts that didn't frighten me. I was not afraid to die, unlikely as that may sound—I had the dreamy curiosity about death that small children have, trying to see if they can hold their breath on and on. And my existence so far had been proof that old cautions didn't hold—I didn't have tracks or a habit or expenses I couldn't afford; I wasn't undernourished and no one was arresting me; I had a job, I was fine. "Look at Bobby," I said.

"Don't get yourself in an uproar," I said, which was Jay's expression. Jay and Nancy did not get along; I had to see them each separately in my off-hours. When I talk to Jay now—we still talk but not often—he seems to remember me as someone who was forever tentative, that is, who made a big show of his reluctance but who had a comically strong appetite. A zany secret glutton, that's Jay's version of me.

I don't think I can explain now how tickled I was with myself at this time. I was glad, not only for the floods of sensation I could call up at will (which I still think of fondly, to be honest), but for the part of the world I had edged into, the layer under the surface that I was now a familiar of. I had always liked walking home from supper in Chinatown at dawn while everyone else was getting ready to go work, and this seemed like that, moving through another city.

Two things happened within a few months of the time I'm talking about: I lost Nancy, and I started to steal from the bar. I might have lost Nancy anyway—she was a lively girl eager to try out her powers—but I neglected her. My days developed a different drama; Nancy seemed less important to me. And I stopped being great shakes in bed, if you want to know the truth. All that was spectacular and precious about Nancy—and is to me still—seemed distant and replaceable to me then. Nancy went back to her Brit boyfriend (she might have been seeing him all along but I prefer not to think so), and I watched him come into the restaurant at night to pick her up after work. In the end he went back to England, and soon after, Nancy took off for London to live with him.

I tried to be a good sport about it, and I even went with her—and about twenty other people from the restaurant—to say goodbye at the airport. Bobby went too. He kept saying, "Shouldn't leave us like this, Miss Nan." The flight didn't take off till three in the morning so we were pretty drunk and wasted by the time she took off—I remember Nancy waving at the gate, a blur of blondness to me—and then we all went for breakfast at one of those plastic airport coffee shops. I had pancakes. At that age I could always eat. When we lined up to pay, the cashier said Bobby had taken care of the checks for all of us. "Oh, no," Donna said. Susan said, "He can't do that. You know how much that cost?" "He wants to," I said. "Let him." And then we all thanked him, much too profusely.

The first and only postcard I sent to Nancy said, "Business downhill since your departure. Customers complain service too polite." My own life was not without variety—I had some girlfriends and I hung out with Jay, who was good at making an evening ceremonious. But I waited for Nancy to write, which she never did. (She sent a card to the whole restaurant—a portrait of Prince Charles as a young chinless nurd, looking remarkably like Alfred E. Newman—and Bobby tacked it over the clam bar.)

The restaurant was losing some of its popularity, as places do, although this took us all by surprise. My tips were not what they had been. Every night Jay and I emptied out the tip cup and made witty remarks about our futures as janitors. I didn't start stealing until I had an increase in my needs, but once I started I wondered why I hadn't done it before. It was easy, and at the end of the night I could go home without feeling mad.

Gordon didn't notice the stealing at first, but he gave me lectures about my appearance. Why did I wear the same cruddy shirt three days in a row? Were my teeth getting worse or what? See that man at table four, Gordon said. He used to be smart and prosperous, but now he's skinny and drugged out and stupid, look at him now. Look, he said.

That was when I thought about the steaks. Steaks were the most expensive things on the menu, and now only Gordon ate them. The chef had bought them fresh but these days they were all stockpiled in the freezer. Nobody knew how many were there. Suppose I could sell a few boxes of them, what would that bring? Jay would know someone to buy them. It was a dumb idea, risky for too little money. I was getting dumb and reckless.

Meanwhile Gordon went around trying to shrink his business losses. He cut back on ordering everything, he bothered all the waitresses about smiling and looking friendly (Donna almost quit over this one), and he made a nuisance of himself in the kitchen over waste control. Bobby would say, "Get that man a vacation," when Gordon left the room. And the restaurant's equipment, which had been bought secondhand, started to give out all at once. The oven got unreliable and burned the roast meats; then the dishwashing machine konked out, and for three nights the staff had to wash everything by hand. I told Bobby that the building was returning to a state of nature. "*The Dismal Swamp*," Bobby said. "*Planet of the Apes*," I said.

At closing time when I was depressed about my finances I went back to contemplate the steaks and count how many were in each box. I looked over the produce too, the butter and milk. The cats watched me, hoping for a handout. By mistake I locked one of them in the walk-in icebox overnight. Bobby said the cat walked out fine the next day, spry and crabby, swishing her tail. But everyone wanted to know who was the jerk who'd been in the refrigerator, and it made me lay low for a while.

For a while I thought about dealing. There were a lot of people close at hand who might be interested in buying; also, if you're a dealer it's good to be findable all the time, and there I was behind the bar. I did need a career advancement. When I talked to Jay about it, he was discouraging—aghast is more like it. He said I'd get caught in about five minutes, stuck in one public spot like a sitting duck.

But I couldn't stop hanging around the steaks. One night I took out a whole box to try to guess their weights—were they really full one-pound sirloins?—the cardboard by this time was thickly frosted and blood-smeared and dank. I heard a footstep near me, and in my panic I actually jumped. It was Reginald, the head cook, and he said, "No good." I thought he meant me, caught in the act, but he meant the steaks. He opened the box and sniffed one of the paper-wrapped hunks, which gave off an odor like a monthlong garbage strike. "This freezer is crap," Reginald said, and for my loitering in the area I got stuck on my break helping him clean the thing out. I smelled rotten when I got back to the bar.

I THOUGHT OF FINDING A JOB at another restaurant. My other plans for my future were vague and childish, and I did not confide them to anyone. One night I went back into the kitchen to scrounge for extra lemons, and when I turned around, I almost tripped over

Bobby, who was in the corner, slumped against a bag of onions, out cold. It was the middle of his shift, for Christ's sake. Donna walked in to place an order, and we both yelled, "Hey, Bobby. Yoohoo. Hey." Donna tapped his shoulder in a fast, scared way, and I shook him. "Bobby, please," I said. "Up, up. Get up."

Very slowly, Bobby raised his head—I could see he didn't know where he was—and then his eyes focused on us. His mouth was slack, his face was still gone. It was hard to watch him. I'd seen enough people like that, dimmed out and adrift in the private shell of the body, but with Bobby it was more than I wanted to see, none of our business. "Shit," he said. He stood up and pulled his apron around. "Caught me napping," he said.

When I told Jay, he went back and had a grim little conference with Bobby, although I couldn't see how Jay had anything useful to say. The rest of us stayed quiet, and it was a bleak night, with long spells of dullness. I was glad Nancy wasn't there to see me, walking up and down the duckboards, making wisecracks, looking for someone to serve. I meant to go back to check on Bobby, but I lost track of time—since Nancy was gone, he didn't stay around after work—and he went home without my knowing.

Bobby started showing up for work late, which always threw Gordon into a panic. Gordon would want to call Bobby at home, and then he'd remember there was no phone number for Bobby, and then he'd mutter about how every worker in the place was robbing him blind, and then Bobby would walk in, looking bothered, complaining about the subway.

One night a woman showed up at the restaurant looking for Bobby. "Bobby's *girl*friend is here," Donna said. We hadn't thought about this side of his life. Why hadn't we? You could get a knowing glance from Bobby if you made a racy remark, but he didn't talk about females himself and he never flirted with the waitresses like some of the other cooks. The woman who came to visit him—she was sitting on a stool in the kitchen when I saw her—was a plain-faced, grumpy person in a cotton dress and flip-flop sandals. We all said, hey, nice to meet you, and she grunted in reply. Bobby was clearly not happy about her being there.

She wasn't leaving either. She stayed through most of the night, not budging from the spot. Bobby walked around muttering. It was plain her visit was part of a longer argument between them. She was there to get money, or to spite him, or to check out this place that was supposed to be so great. When Bobby came to the bar for his scotch, he wouldn't take a drink back for her when I offered. Even Jay kept away from her.

Donna said Bobby was screwing up the food orders tonight. "Who cares?" I said. But we weren't used to seeing him like this. Usually he was patient, above the fray. Remain cool, the evening is young: he was the one who said that. When I went into the kitchen, I made some smart-aleck remarks to Bobby, so the girlfriend would see our usual friendly rhythm, but he was not exactly crackling with backtalk tonight. The woman didn't say a word—I never did hear her speak. Maybe they had lived together for years, maybe they had just met. Bobby's tenderer feelings for her were certainly not evident at this moment, but who knows what they had together? Donna reported overhearing them quarrel, but they stopped when she came into sight.

In the end Bobby did get the girlfriend to leave. She went out through the dining room, tugging her skimpy jacket around her and slapping her sandals against the floor. She still looked mad, so he may not have given her what she made the trip for. (Not that she could've been expected to wave a glassine envelope in the air and shout happily in front of us.) Bobby seemed every bit as irritated after she left. "God*damn*," he'd be saying to himself when anyone walked into the kitchen. We were fading for him, by then.

Slow as business was that night, I kept filching as much money as I could, out of sheer dissatisfaction and itchiness. On the way home from work I made a stop I shouldn't have made, and on the way home from that I must have fallen in the street. I woke up a mess. I was lying in the doorway of a store, in the thin light of early morning, and my head felt as if someone had stepped on it. My hair was stiff with dried blood in the back, and one side of my face was scraped and swollen. Probably I had just hit my head on the sidewalk when I passed out, but I found out someone had gotten my wallet, which frightened me to think of. When I got to my feet, I ran home to my apartment, picking up speed as I went.

I was okay in the morning, but in the afternoon I felt so bad I took myself to the emergency room at St. Vincent's. They told me I had a concussion and put me under observation. Why that is supposed to be such a great hospital is beyond me; the food was lousy and the nurses were mean. The word *detox* was not really popular then, and I was left to my own devices.

Donna and Jay came to visit me, and Donna flirted with me, which was nice of her, considering how I must've looked, a scabby, unshaven goon in a seersucker hospital gown. Jay asked if there was anything I needed—my nose was running like rain, a recognizable sign of how strung out I was—but I'd been through the worst already and the thought of shooting up in the St. Vincent's john really chilled me to the bone. I couldn't stay there long—there was no insurance, nothing like that—but when I got home I didn't go anywhere or eat much and I just stayed inside. I didn't answer my door or my phone.

In my long days at home I would take naps. I dreamed of Nancy and other women I'd been with, and I always woke up happy, despite the absence of real-life women in my house. My old longings made me happy. When my mother called from Toledo, I told her I was having a vacation in my own home. Sometimes my dreams got mixed in with the TV I was watching.

When I went back to the restaurant, Bobby was gone. There was a new second cook in his place. Donna said Bobby had been coming to work later and later, and one day he just didn't show up. No one knew where he was or had a way to find out. Gordon didn't want me back either, as a matter of fact, since my absence had only pointed out whose sticky fingers had been in the till. I was done with that job anyway. I knew that.

I WAS NOT AS READY TO GO ON to other things as I would have thought. I tried bartending in other places, and I did try dealing. My ideas were always circling the same spots. Then I tried brainless jobs—bike messenger, salesman in a T-shirt shop. I was just walking through everything and waiting. All the same, time passed, and now I have a different life.

My daughter, who is eleven and whom I see on weekends, is crazy about horses, and I take her riding from the stables near Central Park. I often think about Bobby when I'm there; I think about running into him while we're both on horseback loping along the trail, our paths crossing in some leafy junction.

I work as a real estate agent—a hard job to have these days, but I keep my head above water. I'm out and around a lot, which I like. For a long while, I used to think I saw Bobby walking toward me in the street; then I would think that by this time Bobby was probably dead. He might be, but why did I think so? What was wrong with my imagination that I couldn't picture his life looping around, getting worse and then better? He had much more experience than I did in leveling off and fucking up all over and getting cleaned up again. He may well be fine. I like to think that he is a cook somewhere, the one profitable thing he got from his time with us.

I have not been to Harlem, except to get a cab from the train station, since I made my trip to 125th Street with Bobby. And wherever Bobby is, I don't think he's downtown. That was then, this is now, as my daughter would say. Bobby, whatever he's doing, is doing it in a separate realm, invisible to me.

It is Nancy who is dead, although I can still sometimes forget this. It seems like a mistake to me, a misreporting. She drowned swimming off the coast of Ibiza. She had been drinking and drifted out too far from shore. A lot of people drink themselves silly on the beach; it still makes me angry that she couldn't afford this particular bit of stupidity. I feel she should have been allowed more than that, Nancy of all people.

I don't know how she would have liked the decade of her forties, which for me has been very good. I notice that I've become someone who takes great private pleasure in things around me. On some days my own apartment seems like a vale of peace and light. My daughter is growing into this amazing creature; she's a sharp girl, terrifically smart. She thinks I am a flake and definitely a bit much in public. I have habits left over from being a bartender. I joke with people I don't know; I get into gabby exchanges with people in stores, much to my daughter's mortification. I am a curious, sometimes clumsy person. I understand that in many ways I have been very lucky in my life.

Lake Natasink

When Patty comes in to work on her second-to-last day, Jack is sitting in her office. In her chair, naturally. It isn't really an office, just a partitioned area in the big, messy room they use for Administration. Her stall, she's always called it. "Look hard," Jack says. "This is what you leave behind when you abandon Manhattan."

"How can I bear it?" Patty says.

"Don't beg any of us to send you cockroaches," Jack says. "Don't call any of us in the middle of the night and plead with us to talk dirty."

Carmen comes in from Client Records. "Look at her," Jack says, pointing to Patty. "Miss Rustic. Miss Farmer Jones." Patty is wearing a purple leopard-print turtleneck, the same sort of thing she always wears. So what?

"They got wild animals in the country," Carmen says. "Right?"

"Not as wild as me," Patty says. "Jack thinks I might be too much for them upstate."

"I hope so," Carmen says, and leaves with a folder.

"What will you eat?" Jack says. "Velveeta? Twinkies? Spam? Go ahead, tell me Spam is great. Baked with canned pineapple and Karo syrup."

"Spam is great," Patty says.

"You know how much weight you'll put on?" Jack says. "In a week you'll look like a Twinkie yourself."

Being Jack, he is looking for the spot where he'll get to her, but he hasn't found it yet. Weight isn't it. When she first moved in with Charlotte, Jack made fat jokes every time he saw Patty eat a cookie. She was going to get fat from Charlotte's cooking, he decided. Overstuffed on pâté and profiteroles. Charlotte, Patty's lover, is a trained chef. Patty isn't fat. She is five two and weighs a hundred and four pounds, sometimes a hundred and five. Her hair, which is in a crewcut, is currently hennaed a winey color. She has holes pierced for three earrings in one ear and she uses them all. She's forty-two—okay, a little old for that sort of thing—but she's not ready to change. She looks fine.

It's Jack who doesn't look so good. He looks craggy and blown out, like an old junkie, which he is. He never did look that great. He and Patty have known each other since they were in their twenties. He was notably unvain about himself then—at least about his looks—but he could get women when he wanted to. Actually anybody could, at that time. But he and Patty were never a couple. They were cronies.

He liked to dare her to do things; he would goad or mock or coax or lure her if she tried to turn back. It was exciting—you never knew what you would end up doing if you were with Jack. Some things she would rather forget; some things she remembers with amazement and probably pride. They were the most she would do, the furthest she would go. At the time she was grateful to Jack.

For many years they didn't see each other. Jack was in Miami, she was in New York. He had a family, a whole other life, in Florida. When he called her, she wasn't always happy to hear from him. His voice on the line always startled her: "This is Jack, the one and only." And now he and Charlotte don't get along—and who can blame Charlotte? But their baby, Wyona, loves him. Wyona shrieks with excitement when Jack comes into the room. She holds out her arms—she wants him to swing her around, to hold her upside down by her feet. Sometimes he tosses her up and catches her. Charlotte can't stand it. Wyona squeals and laughs. She begs for more. "Airplane girl," Jack says. "Little flying woman."

At work people seem to like him so far. Patty got him this job. He's training to be an assistant counselor in the drug treatment program at the Center. He has seven years' sobriety, which counts as a credential here. Patty guesses he's lying about when his last slip was, but they probably know that. If they don't who does? Patty herself is only the office manager, at second remove from what she calls the real dirty work of the Center. If the place weren't so underfunded and chaotic, it would be a calming job.

Anyway it's her next-to-last day. All week she has been forgetting that she's leaving—a sign, she assumes, that she doesn't want to go. It's Lake Natasink, New York, that she and Charlotte and the baby are moving to, and all week Jack has been calling it Lake Kitchen Sink. Patty tries to think of the house they'll be living in—the front porch, the view of fields and hills from the back. The reasons she wants to be there. The quiet, the relief. When Jack says she'll go nuts from boredom, she says, "I can't wait."

"Tell me what you'll do with yourself all day," Jack says. "Check to see if your manure pile is decomposing? Read seed catalogues?"

In fact she will have plenty to do—she has a job at a state agency in Albany (there's more substance abuse up there than you would think) and she has Wyona. Also the house needs work. Maybe Jack still thinks of her as idle and slow. When she was young she could sleep till two in the afternoon, after a late night. She could read one page of the paper, eat a chocolate donut, and feel the day was well spent. Her whole sense of time was different then. She wore tiny silk tank tops in the dead of winter, heavy cowboy boots in August.

"A lot of people don't want to be in New York," Jack says. "You have to have guts to stay here. You might like it better upstate."

"Thank you so much," Patty says.

She reminds Jack that when he lived in Miami he couldn't believe someone like herself still put up with crappy winter weather and no place to park and no beach. Why didn't she move down there, he wanted to know, what did she have in New York that was so great?

Patty still has the photos he sent her: Jack waving a conch shell, Jack with a banana in his ear, Jack pretending to scale a palm tree. He worked for a while as a disco manager, a job that got interrupted when he beaned himself falling off a pier at midnight. Sometimes Patty tells him his head is still flat on one side. "It's my hip haircut," he says, "copied by millions." Actually he is quite bald now.

But now he likes New York again. Now he wants her to be in New York the way he is. How come he can't have an opinion, Patty says, without selling it to everyone he knows?

So if I were like you, Patty thinks, I'd be cooking chili over a hot plate in a residence hotel, how great is that? She has said this to him—they have said everything to each other—but at the moment she is starting to think she will miss him.

"Hey, Jack," she says. "Move up there yourself. Get into goat-herding or something."

"I've been low," Jack says, "but not that low." But his face brightens. It's always nice to be invited. In his own way he looks up to her and Charlotte, the happy homemakers.

Patty feels glad that at least she's leaving him in this job, useful work in a place he won't quit. There are a lot of crappy agencies, but Patty thinks this isn't one of them. Legit people work here and Patty has seen some pretty whacked-out clients get better. You can't ever guess which ones; the dark horses surprise you, the favorites fade out.

While she's talking to Jack, a workman comes in to move her desk. They'll be reshuffling offices after she leaves. "What the hell are you doing?" Jack says. "She's still working. You want her to sit on the floor?"

The man is lifting the desk, papers and all. Maybe the young lady can sit in the reception area instead.

"Come back Monday," Patty says. "Okay?"

"Get out of here," Jack says. "I mean it."

For a moment Patty thinks a little brawl is going to break out. The workman is getting red. But he drops the desk hard, acts disgusted with them, and walks out. Patty's always liked it when Jack gets chivalrous.

"You're not fucking gone yet," he says.

THE REST OF THE DAY Patty works on making lists for her successor. Her job has mostly involved billing the clients' insurance companies, if they have them. Someone has to pay for this.

The lists keep getting longer, and she is tired by the time she goes home. In their apartment Charlotte has the boxes out for packing. There is maybe a square foot of empty floor space, and one of the cats is already hiding in panic. They have three cats and a dog. The baby is eleven months old and just starting to walk. One glance at their apartment—even without the boxes—and it's obvious they should move to the country, or somewhere.

The baby loves the empty boxes. Charlotte has tipped one on its side for her and she's busy crawling in and out of it. "Wyona the famous infant explorer," Charlotte says. The baby's mother, who had her for the first three months of her life, named her Wyona, and they promised to keep the name. Wyona's mother is black and her father is Korean. Jack has pointed out that she will have a lot of explaining to do in kindergarten about how those two white dykes are Mom and Mom. That and getting people to spell her name right (Wyona Szasznec-Stein)—this kid has a number of challenges ahead of her.

You wouldn't know it watching her clamber around the boxes. To see her makes Patty think about the blind stupidity of youth, the blithe stubbornness of it. She is thinking of the year she and Jack and a lot of other people used to go to Central Park at dawn after they'd been up all night. They walked down the paths in the dim sepia light; they watched the sky get brighter behind the bushes. It *was* beautiful, probably. Once near Bethesda Fountain they ran into a group of Asian men in kimonos practicing some martial art. Patty remembers everyone watching and laughing silently in amazement. Later they heard noises in the Ramble, but no one bothered them. *The Ramble*? The Ramble wasn't safe in broad daylight. What did they think they were doing?

The baby has gotten her foot caught in her own pants leg and is making a fussy, crying noise, a whimper that is the beginning of a louder complaint. "Goofball," Charlotte says. "Are you thinking about crying? Think again." Of all of them, the one who has changed the most is Charlotte. She is so stunned by the good luck of getting this baby that she is incredibly cheerful. She walks down the street with her bright blue stroller, making up rhymes out loud. She is sunny and competent. She claims taking care of a baby is easy, something Patty has never heard anyone say before and knows to be untrue. Babies tell you what they want, Charlotte says, their needs are simple.

"Five of the boxes are for you," Charlotte says. Patty is a little behind on her packing, to put it mildly. It is pretty open between them that she is starting to get cold feet about going. Just lately it seems like too much trouble to her to try to start all over in a new place. At her age. Why should this be asked of her? She doesn't offer this as any sort of argument. She believes in fresh starts, in second chances, in tremendous shifts at any age, any stage. She works in a treatment center, doesn't she?

All the same, she thinks Charlotte is leaning on her too hard about this, rushing her, bullying her even. Let Charlotte pack all the cartons if she wants to get out of here so goddamned fast. Patty doesn't say this. She says, "Maybe my stuff will just fly into the boxes, and the boxes will fly into the car."

"Sure," Charlotte says. "Don't budge and you'll find out."

Patty watches the baby, who is quietly chewing on a corner of the box, while Charlotte begins dinner preparations. Even now, Charlotte doesn't believe in meals that are too hasty and unceremonious. The kitchen begins to smell of garlic, butter, onions, cheese. Sometimes Patty still can't believe she eats like this every night.

When Jack came to dinner the first time, he made fun of their kitchen—the salt-grinder, the hanging wreaths of peppers (hilarious props, to hear him tell it)—but he was a little different around Patty after that, more eager, even somewhat chastened.

The baby has cornered the dog and is pulling at the fur on his neck. The dog looks patient and miserable, but who knows what his breaking point is? He's a big dog, a collie-shepherd mix they found in the street. Patty pries Wyona away and the baby shrieks in protest.

She lets out a series of really loud squawks and by the time Patty distracts her with the Kermit doll, Charlotte wants the salad washed.

"We won't get arugula like this upstate," Patty says.

"Of course we will. In our garden. Bill has it in his. He has radicchio too." Bill is their one friend in the area.

"He loves his garden," Patty says. "That's all he talks about now. Except in winter. In winter he's into chimney maintenance."

"He needs to have that thing relined," Charlotte says. To Charlotte all of this is cozy and lively.

"And he's obsessed about landfills. Mr. Garbage. A dinner with him feels like it's about two days long."

"Don't go next time then."

"You'll get like that soon. You'll be like him."

Patty knows that she is being spiteful and sour and that her reasons for doing this are weak and unsound. Why is she doing this? Curdling what happiness they have, trying to spoil her own luck, which she must know by now is hard to come by. She is riled up anyway, full of hot indignation at whatever she thinks Charlotte is doing to them, to her.

Patty sees them in the future, meek, stout, spinsterish. On the porch of their farmhouse. Talking about their attic insulation. They will have forgotten what they knew of anything aberrant, expansive, or emotionally subterranean. They will have made themselves forget.

"You were always like that actually," Patty says.

That starts them both up. Once they get going they won't stop. They dig up the worst evidence about each other they can remember, the most enraging details. Why are they together, then? Patty thinks it is all a mistake. She feels hard and clear and slightly out of her mind.

In their new clarity they shout scathing advice to each other. Their voices frighten, not Wyona, who is sleeping by now and who sleeps through everything, but the dog. He thinks they are yelling at him. He runs to hide under the sofa, scrambling to fit himself under the frame. "It's okay, Freddie," Patty says. "Good dog, good Fredster." Patty's voice, which Charlotte can hear too, is cajoling and sweet; it makes all the squabbling between them seem fake and affected, a phony harshness. Charlotte comes over; together they offer the dog a piece of cheese. Freddie edges out and makes a fast lunge for it. Then he backs under the sofa again.

After this they are both somewhat embarrassed about fighting. They set the meal on the table as if some rude outside person had interrupted the proper urgency of eating. They sit down quietly. They watch the news.

On TV there are wounded soldiers in a hospital. Patty can't believe they watch this while they eat. At the end there is a spot feature on an English rock group's tour of Russia. The camera shows them blowing out one of their amplifiers, which makes Charlotte laugh. Charlotte was a drummer in a woman's rock band for a few years. They toured as far as Oregon; they cut one record. Charlotte still has her old T-shirts with the group's name in crusty silver letters. She teaches Wyona percussive effects with spoons and cake pans; she has bought her a set of claves. There is nothing wrong with Charlotte.

When the baby wakes up cranky they offer her apple juice, but it takes a while to get her back to sleep. Charlotte, who has been doing most of the Wyona work all day, goes off to bed early. Patty still hasn't done the boxes.

She walks the dog, who is thrilled to be out. On the street he barks at a couple out jogging. People have been jogging for some time, but it still strikes Patty as something you would never do if you didn't live in this particular era. A whole generation of people is rigorously athletic through a kind of historical fate, Patty thinks.

You could say drugs were like that twenty years ago. People who wouldn't have been anywhere near them in another time used them freely as a matter of course, developed appetites and kinds of slyness they wouldn't have known they had.

Not Jack, though. Jack would've been into something no matter when he was born, something shady and sporty and hidden. Jack is more of an old tricky type, a perennial. At present he is trying to figure out how to harass Patty about her move and at the same time foster a mutual assumption that he is welcome to stay with them in the country any time. He is much better than he used to be.

He used to be much less mild in his little jokey personal remarks; once he started he didn't stop. Patty has seen people throw bottles at him in sheer anguish. But he has always liked Patty—she thinks—been more careful with her than with other people. He flattered her, at least. That's our girl, he would say, to talk her into things. Anyway she liked this.

Something else Patty doesn't forget is that Jack once stood by her all night when she was waiting for a girlfriend to show up from California and the girlfriend got mysteriously delayed for twenty-four hours. He made Patty play a very long game of Monopoly, and they watched *Sunrise Semester* together on TV. He was good at making people do things, a skill Patty admired this one time. And he could juggle—he had learned somewhere or taught himself. It was funnier than you would think to see him throwing oranges around. He looked so intent and hardworking and yet so light, so wacky. That night he juggled blueberries, a big mess.

So Patty owed him for this; she is an honorable person or tries to be. She lent him money when he asked, she didn't mind. He borrowed ten dollars and gave it back the next week. Who minds that? Then he borrowed again and had trouble paying her back, and he had to keep borrowing. His accumulated debt with her went up to a hundred, worth more then but not exactly a fortune. And he seemed truly embarrassed every time he asked, sorry that he had come to this. "It's fine," she would tell him. What she hated was seeing him so shamed and apologetic. Or did she?

Jack was working in a record store—getting a salary that had always been enough before—so his habit must've grown by a few leaps. (Within a year he took off for Florida to try to cut back, but Patty didn't put these things together till later.) One day a man bought some albums with a MasterCard and forgot to take it back when he left. It made Jack happy to have found a way to pay her back.

Everything wasn't on computers then. Stores made phone calls to check credit card numbers but Jack said that if you bought something under a certain amount nobody bothered. What did Patty need for twenty dollars or less? She could pick it out herself; they would go shopping. Whatever she wanted.

Gloves, Patty said right away. It was winter and she kept losing them. She was down to a ratty red wool pair with holes. Leather ones would be nice, lined leather. Wool or fur lining, she didn't care.

When they walked into the department store Patty felt normal. As normal as she felt most of the time in those days. She was used to doing things that surprised her; she was interested in what she would do. It so happened this wasn't the sort of adventure that especially thrilled her, but then here she was.

It was a small department store, and the saleswoman didn't have a big range of gloves to show them. "Just something plain," Patty said. She had to settle for ones with funny brass fasteners, the plainest they had. "You sure you like them?" Jack said. "Get what you like."

The gloves were fourteen dollars. The saleswoman, who was young and unfriendly, took the card and picked up a phone near her cash register. Right away Jack caught Patty's eye. He tilted his head—was that a signal to go? The woman spoke over the phone in a chatty normal way, probably just tallying the amount with some bureau in the store. Patty started drifting away from the counter, looking at displays, and then she drifted back, not wanting to panic. "God," she called to Jack, "they make you go through so much red tape now." Jack was an aisle away, but he came back to her then.

Patty browsed around the mittens, waiting. And then she saw Jack start running. Patty remembers the sudden sight of his back, his elbows moving up and down. The saleswoman, in her high heels, was after him—she was shouting, "Security guard! Stop this man!" as if she'd been trained to say that. Patty remembers being stunned that this was happening in a department store, with the stupid musical bells of elevators and the hum of shoppers around them. What she doesn't remember now is whether she saw the guard when he got Jack. She kept her distance, moving through the displays like any customer, strolling toward the door, and she remembers the rush of thankfulness when she was out on the street. But she must have seen him caught. She didn't wait for him by the door or across the street, which she would've done otherwise.

But Patty knew right away it had been her fault. She saw then how she wasn't cut out for this sort of thing, had no business being there. All her calmness, her clever guessing, had been completely off the mark. And Jack paid for it.

But what could they do to him for fourteen dollars worth of fraud? In fact they did a lot to him. For one thing, he had racked up a few other purchases on the card. Even so. Perhaps it just took two days to arraign him and no one could get him out before then. Maybe he didn't call a lawyer. He spent two days in the Tombs, the old jail on Centre Street.

Jack called her a few hours after he got out. "It was an unusual experience," he said. He meant that only half as a joke. "I met some fairly interesting people," he said. That was all. He was much less surprised about all of it than she was, and he wasn't angry.

"If I hadn't made us stay," Patty said, "you could've gotten out of the store with no trouble. You wouldn't have gotten arrested if I had let us just leave."

"Patty," he said. "One thing about jail. Every single person has that story. It's full of guys who wouldn't have been there at all if something else had been different. Believe me."

She felt childish then, with her little squeaky protestations. Jack was beyond her. He was way past her just then. And he was very nice to her under the circumstances—gallant, in his way. "Forget it," he said.

PATTY HAS TALKED ABOUT THIS STORY hardly at all. Charlotte knows only a watered-down version. It was a few years before it struck her how truly bumbling she had been—most twelve-year-olds would have been more savvy. So why had Jack wanted to bring her along? He might have done his shopping without her. But he was always bringing people along. He liked getting everyone on his bus; he was a junkie.

Charlotte has said that the story shows how mild and compliant Patty was then. But Patty knows that she was wildly confident, quite full of herself. Never, never did she think they were in any real peril. Why would they be? They thought people who worked in stores were the timid, foolish ones. The things she bothered to worry over then (some of them hair-raising, now that she thinks of them) turned out fine and had no consequences.

Patty can be thankful for that and sometimes she is. All things considered, she has fared well. And lately, with Wyona, her life has taken a turn she could never have expected. When the baby tries to walk now, she grabs hold of Patty's leg and wants to use it as a crutch; if Patty tows her along, she grunts and pants in glee and concentration.

Patty thinks of a city populated by what Charlotte calls born-again families, people startled by late (but not too late) home lives. Who knew they were going to end up like this? Not Patty.

When Patty gets into bed, she looks at Charlotte twisted in the covers. It is a joke between them that they like each other best when they're sleeping, but Patty does have moments of great contentment at this time of night, the sense of floating in some pulsing bright element that is her own real life.

Patty falls asleep like this, but she wakes up when she hears Wyona crying from the living room. Patty believes in stopping her before she really gets going, since she's old enough to stand up and rock the crib once she's in her yowling mode. Charlotte is still asleep or pretending to be.

"Who's crying?" Patty says, when she goes in to her. "That's some other baby, that's not Wyona." The baby wails a little more and then when Patty starts the music box (it's a mobile that plays "Somewhere over the Rainbow"), Wyona listens and pipes down.

Patty hasn't told Charlotte she got this child-care tip from Jack, of all people. Charlotte would decide it was a corrupt device if she knew. As it is, she is thinking of buying a giant bear from Toys R Us that plays "Für Elise."

Jack has two children in Miami, two boys. They're thirteen and fifteen. His wife doesn't want him to see them. When they were little, he took them with him sometimes to his dealer's house; it was a stop he had to make and there was a yard for them to play in. Eileen, his wife, was working at the time. Nothing happened to them in the dealer's yard—the kids remember a woman with a broken tooth who used to be very nice to them—but Eileen has not forgotten this and a number of other things. Eileen is still in Miami, or right outside it. Jack met her there. They lived in a tract house on a canal. To Jack, who is from Detroit, it was the wilderness. They had bougainvillea, hibiscus, star jasmine. There were fish in the canal—once a barracuda, a small one. It was interesting to see, Jack says. He liked the lizards, the pelicans, herons. Even the dolphin show at the aquarium, which his kids insisted on going to about forty times. But he wasn't so sorry to leave, and it's better for everyone if he doesn't go back.

The next day at work there's a farewell party for Patty at the end of the afternoon. Carmen and Darryl, who runs the switchboard, have made a sign that says ESCAPE FROM NEW YORK and Lurene, the clerk supervisor, has brought in her famous carrot cake. Patty is excited by all the attention, by the niceness of people. What a great office she works in. Why is she leaving it? Gail, one of the social workers, says she envies Patty. Gail had her purse stolen last week, out of this very office, and she says she's tired of wasting so much of her life being irritated. "I yell at my husband, I yell at salespeople. I get in line for everything and I'm ready to hit someone. At least I don't come in and yell at the clients." Yelling at the Center's clients is a definite no-no, as is a sarcastic tone or any humor at their expense; plain scolding is okay. One of them probably stole her purse, although it could have been the cleaning lady. Gail is a sweet-faced, high-voiced woman, and if she really is getting shrewish it's a waste (among the other wastes around them.)

Carmen says everything bad that people say about New York is true but she wants to know, where else can you run around all night and you have a dozen different clubs that are worth going to? All right, say only ten. Carmen is in her twenties, going strong.

Gail says, "In the country you won't have to step over garbage in the street." This reminds them all of Willie McIntyre, a client who died of AIDS. He liked to sweep the sidewalk in front of the Center; he was outraged by New York sanitation. The staff once got him a T-shirt that said "Next to Godliness." He was Gail's client; no wonder she says she wants to hide in Patty's luggage when she leaves.

Someone passes around paper cups of 7-Up (no alcohol here). There's a wrapped present the size of a Great Dane—probably a joke, something smaller inside—but Patty is stalling on opening it. Where is Jack, for instance?

The Center's director, Big Bad Brad, is here. Actually he's not a bad guy for a psychiatrist. At present he is ignoring the fact that Marcus and Ernestine have joined the festivities. They are clients in the residential program and they tend to walk the halls and go where they don't belong. Into these offices, for example. Marcus is handsome and chatty, and Ernestine has a bad limp and is scared of things, and neither of them can stand still.

"You got the right idea," Marcus says to Patty. "Leave now before it all falls down. I think I feel some of that debris right now."

"How is she going to get along without us?" Ernestine says. She looks tickled with herself for having made a joke.

Someone has given Patty a foil paper tiara to wear, as if it were New Year's Eve. She feels giddy and sentimental and horrible about leaving. She could stay. It's not too late to ask for her resignation back. It would be embarrassing but no one would mind; they're used to oddness here.

But Patty knows why she's going. All along the whole thing has been her idea as much as Charlotte's. She wants to be in the mountains; she wants, among other things, to be able to see farther than she has. She is sorry sometimes (when she's in the mood to be sorry) that she used up so many years in smallness, in narrow satisfactions and narrow complaints.

The lake they will be living near has mists on it in the morning. From above, when they go hiking, the lake looks like an illusion, a glare of sun in the middle of trees. There it is; no, it isn't—they keep losing it and sighting it. A patch of light along the ground. The first time Charlotte walked along the bank, holding Wyona, Patty saw them from a hundred feet away as if they were made out of dust motes and air, pure figures.

Now Darryl is busy taking pictures of everyone. Patty and Lurene and Gail and Lester all pose with their fingers behind each other's head for horns. And Jack is here finally. "Hey," he says. "It's the party of the season. Someone's going to O.D. on the flavored seltzer any minute."

"Eat your potato chips and be good," Patty says.

Jack is dapper today—he's been uptown visiting the other center, and he's wearing a sports jacket that makes him look like a rock promoter. Even skinny and old he looks a hell of a lot better than he used to. He doesn't even smoke now—he gave that up when he found out he was so good at renouncing. He takes megavitamins, and he jogs twenty miles a week. (Some people don't know when to stop, Patty tells him.)

Patty worries that he's too thin, but he got an HIV test again last month and he was fine. Everyone in the office is always warning Carmen about using condoms, but Patty knows she doesn't listen. She's too young, too vain, too something to want to think about consequences. Now Patty thinks about them all the time. Some days she can hardly move for worrying about what she's doing and what it will do to Wyona. Your heart gets heavier: she once said that to Jack.

"Nice tiara," Jack says. "Going somewhere?"

"She's going to the woods," Marcus says. "To the Garden of Eden."

"With others of her kind," Jack says.

Nobody asks what he means by this. Some of them know about Charlotte and some don't. Is that what he means?

"Going off with the moles and the raccoons," Jack says. "Isn't she?"

"She's no mole," Ernestine says.

"Sure she is," Jack says. He chuckles as if this really were funny.

Jack should be careful, Patty thinks. They like her here, they only sort of like him. They don't know what to make of him. Who does?

Brad wants to know when the hell she's going to open her present. Does she think they just got it for decoration or what? Patty starts ripping through the wrapping paper—it's got tissue under it, and when she unwinds it all she sees they've bought her a rocking chair. It's a nice one, plain, with a walnut finish. "For your retirement," Jack says, which is just what she's saying to herself—how old do these people think she is? Who picked this? But actually she's always liked rocking chairs and it'll be nice for holding Wyona. She goes around kissing everybody to thank them. "Wear it well," Gail says.

"You like the red cushion? You could get blue instead," Darryl says.

"I think it's perfect," Jack says. "Your speed."

"Want a little cake, Jack?" Lurene says. "Keep your mouth full."

Brad says maybe they should move the whole Center to the country. "I wish," he says. He was on TV a month ago talking about how it's going to be when the crack babies grow up. He sounded grave and tired, a doctor giving bad news. They're still teasing him here about his video fame. The show was called "What If New York Can't Be Saved?"—a title the whole staff hated. "Too whiny," Lester said. "Tears in your beer."

Patty is trying out her rocking chair. "God, it's so soothing," she says. "I love it."

"This is what people like to do all the time in the country," Jack says. "All the people who can't move fast enough for New York."

Patty doesn't think she's a failure, but she thinks of how she might really be seen that way. She's stayed just an office worker; she's never pushed herself, as her mother says. Pushed where? Patty always says. Only she sometimes thinks if she had taken a different path they would have more money for Wyona.

"Lake Gutless, that's where you're moving," Jack says.

"Chill out, Jack," Gail says.

"The real people are staying," Jack says. "You're not going anywhere, right, Gail?"

"Not at the moment."

"They don't even have subways up there, that's how uncivilized they are. No Donald Trump. It's a desert. You're not thinking of buying the lot next to her, are you?"

Gail is laughing a little. He has her laughing.

"I didn't think so," Jack says. "You know how I can tell? By your breasts. No one has breasts in Albany. There's no sexual activity of any kind there. Not that Patty has normal sex anyway. She'll be okay in her little shack in the backwoods."

"That's enough," Gail says.

Jack gives one of his slow smiles and holds up his hands. Then he puts his arm around Patty. "She loves me," he says to Gail.

Patty says, "Why are you being such an incredible pain today?"

"Appreciate me," Jack says. "Soon you'll be off with the rabbits and the moles."

"She's not a mole," Ernestine says.

"Sure she is," Jack says.

Ernestine shakes her head.

"What do you know about it?" Jack says. "You don't know anything. You don't even know how to spell *mole*, do you? Spell it for me. I'd like to hear you."

The room is quiet, and Brad is looking at Jack with his famous evil eye. Jack is giving him a return stare. "Relax, Big B.," he says. "You look like a raccoon just goosed you." Jack is going to get himself fired, Patty thinks. If not now then later. What did she get him this job for then?

Ernestine is busy walking around the room in a zigzag, skittering like a cockroach. She probably does know how to spell, she just doesn't know how to talk most of the time. Jack still has his arm around Patty. What are they doing stuck together like this? Patty thinks everyone in the room must be asking that question. What's the longest she's gone without seeing Jack? Oh, years, and they could go that long again. Easy. Sometimes he just looks like some bald stranger.

Ernestine is stomping against the floor with her cane. She has never done this before, and Patty can't tell if it's nervous or menacing. "I guess you're applauding me," Jack says. Marcus is hovering around.

Meanwhile Jack is pinching Patty's waist. "Too many chocolate donuts," he says, about a food she hasn't eaten in fifteen years.

And then Jack does something Patty doesn't expect. He goes over to the carrot cake and cuts a piece. "Hey, Ernestine," he says. "I hear there's drugs hidden in this. Better grab a piece fast before it all goes." Ernestine looks wary, but she sits down and eats a piece when he gives it to her. Jack picks up Ernestine's cane. "You got your weapon here," he says. "So I better watch out." He twirls it around; he swings it in big circles like a dancer in a chorus number. He throws it behind his back and tries to catch it from between his knees, but he drops it. He looks merry and clumsy, bouncier than you would think. Ernestine is laughing with her hand over her mouth.

See that? Patty wants to say to the room. Look at that. She is jealous in advance of everything that will go on without her. Look at Jack leaping around. Patty wants to ask him what vitamins he takes. She isn't even packed yet. How does anyone move? All the same, she'll be out of here soon, ready or not.

Without Ellie

I.

Whenever Ellie came for supper, it was hard to know what she would eat. By that spring, we had been stepsisters for ten years, and over that time I'd seen her avoid and prefer a great range of foods. One night she said the meal was really good, but she mostly worked on the sautéed string beans, and she had two pieces of chocolate cake for dessert. I tried to get her to take a third.

"I ate a lot already," Ellie said. "Don't worry."

For years I'd tried to talk other people out of worrying about Ellie. Ellie was fine—what was fine anyway? Ellie's brother, who hardly saw her anymore, used to ask me, is she better or is she getting crazy again? He said crazy as a cut-off term, and I had my times of feeling it that way too: you're crazy, don't bother me.

Ellie's mother used to call and ask me whether I'd seen Ellie lately. How was she, how did she look? "She looked fine to me," I'd say. I could always hear that pause on the other line. *Oh, to you.*

This time Ellie did look healthy at least. She wasn't too skinny any more; in fact she was getting softly fat, baby-round for someone in her twenties. She was dressed lumpy—she had on a full wool skirt and an embroidered peasant blouse over a red sweater. Her hair, always blonde and bushy, looked dryly clean.

But it bothered me that she wasn't eating more protein for dinner. I was never sure what Ellie lived on, in any sense. She didn't work for a living. Her father, Stanley (my stepfather, a nice enough guy), must've been giving her money, but how much? Sometimes Ellie talked about wanting to do things—for a while she was going to work for a florist or be a guard in a museum—but it was increasingly hard to imagine her following directions or sitting at a desk. I thought it was a bad cycle: not doing anything, not being able to, waiting to be able to. I'd held (if you could use that word) a long list of jobs myself—Xerox machine operator, hand model, mail-order processor, waitress.

"The cake is good, huh?" I said. "It's from the restaurant." Doug, the man I lived with, owned a small restaurant, which I sort of managed. It was a local hangout bar, near where we lived on the Lower East Side, and it had occasional touches of elegance on the menu; this was *reine de Saba.*

"You could be a baker, couldn't you?" Ellie said. "You could make this yourself, you could bake at home."

"I'm already employed."

"You'd be better off in the kitchen," Ellie said. "It would be better for you. You know what I mean."

Ellie believed that I swam in a sea of corruption. She thought I needed to stay home to be safe or good. For herself too, she could only imagine a few ways to be out of harm's way.

"I know what you do for a job," she said. "You stand around not giving a shit about anything. Your job is to let everybody see you doing that."

"Imagine getting paid for that," I said. "Lucky me. Go be a baker yourself."

It turned out that Ellie did have a new idea for a job she might want. She could be a mail carrier. She was a great walker and she never got tired, she said. (This was true.) I thought her mother, Roslyn, would have a fit when she heard this, but I said, "Terrific, a very good idea."

What Ellie did all day anyway was walk around, all over the city. Up Eighth Avenue all the way to Inwood, down Park Avenue to across the Brooklyn Bridge. Stopping only for a fast pretzel from a vendor, as if she were a hiker with a trail to cover. She roved into any neighborhood and no one bothered her.

In high school, when Ellie used to visit her father, she spent half the weekends taking long rambling walks on suburban Long Island. She would come home tired out, with dry twigs sticking to her coat. In the dead of winter she sometimes wore only Indian buffalo sandals—she said she minded the cold but she was too lazy to change.

When my mother got married to Stanley, I was just out of college, or as much college as I'd stayed in for. On those weekends when Ellie and I were both visiting the parental house, I went on some of those walks with her. We crossed through acres of houses and yards; we went to a marsh with cattails and brambles. And in the evenings we would go off to the basement together and smoke dope. Ellie liked to whisper about getting wrecked in the rec room—she was only fifteen, that was sly wit to her. Once I braided Ellie's hair into cornrows; I wove into the braids everything that was within reach—string, metal washers, Scotch tape, strips of wrapping paper.

We could hardly stand our own brilliance. Ellie wanted her picture taken. She said she wanted to remember herself that way. Bo Derek meets Bride of Frankenstein. When we went upstairs to show off, my mother said, "Very sophisticated. Two mature adults here." "The nut sisters," Stanley said.

But I liked this mail-carrying idea, as I thought about it. Ellie would have a steady purpose, a fixed route, a daily routine. And she wanted to do it; it was so rare that she wanted to do anything. I got happy thinking about it. "You could be the first person in history to bring mail on time to New York apartments," I said. I threw my arms around her. "Girl warrior of the postal system."

Ellie said, "It's an idiot job. I know that. I'm a lunatic, not an idiot."

"Never mind," I said. "Everybody has to work."

In fact Ellie had not had to work, so far. Sometimes at the end of the night at the restaurant, when I was exhausted and fed up with every customer in the place, I thought about Ellie not working and it offended my sense of justice.

"Come work at the post office with me," Ellie said.

From the beginning, she had never liked the work I did in restaurants. She had strong principles, and in her own way she acted on them. My mother had found her pony-skin purse floating in the bathtub; Stanley had found a charred copy of *Sports Illustrated* on his pillow. Ellie was disturbed when I first started waitressing. My mother was disturbed too, but she was my mother and not used to blithe downward mobility. It was Ellie who said, "Oh, you won't stop now. In those pants you wear." I wore cigarette jeans, all the rage that year. "I'm doing my best not to stop," I told her. "My very best."

So Ellie put on my black taffeta apron and a clear plastic raincoat over her underwear, and she paraded around the living room in high heels. "Recognize this person?" she said. "This is you." "What a dish," I said. "Can that hot young thing really be me?" Ellie took off the raincoat and the apron, took off her white cotton bra and bikinis, lay down on the floor with her knees up. "Cut it out," her father said. "Go upstairs if you're going to be funny."

It always amazed me that Ellie thought her advice would convert me. She must have thought that a sting of understanding would run through me, and I would get it at last. She was very certain about her opinions; she was burning up with certainty.

"Doug wants you to stay there, doesn't he?" Ellie said now. "In the restaurant. I know he does."

Doug, my boyfriend, did his best to get along with Ellie. As a saloonkeeper, he was unfazed by most kinds of human behavior. What could Ellie do that would shake him? Stand on her head, get down on all fours and bark? A mere conversational waviness or a religious streak was nothing to him. Also Doug was nice. In niceness he listened to Ellie; he cocked his head, he waited for her to be done.

"You do whatever Doug says," Ellie said. "You follow his every word."

"Never," I said. "Can we get on another topic? Can we talk about the weather?"

"It's going to be a cooler summer than usual," Ellie said. "*The Farmer's Almanac* said. Usually they're right."

It caught me by surprise that she really had switched topics. Usually she dug in once she got started.

"Nice for you if you're working outside," I said.

"I'll get a tan," she said. "I'll be unbelievably stunning, in my gray uniform."

She *is* better, I thought. She's much better. I was ashamed that I had not allowed for this, in all my wary guesses about Ellie's future. I tried to imagine an Ellie getting older, frizzy-haired and daffy, a maiden eccentric. Full of loopy opinions and odd habits, but one of us, a cohabitant of the usual world. The thought knocked me out: my friend again, given back.

And really the worst time had been quite a while ago, several years ago. She was much better since then. On a bus from Portland, Maine, to New York, Ellie had taken off all her clothes. She had gone into the bathroom on the bus and come out naked. Then she'd sat quietly in a seat, talking a little to herself but not bothering anybody. Someone had gone up to the driver and told him and he had stopped the bus and made everyone else get off, and later an ambulance had come for Ellie. They took her off the bus wrapped in a blanket. When I'd gone to visit her in the nut ward, Ellie had more or less laughed about the whole thing—her "nudist Trailways trip." She was not defiant about it, but she joked as she might have about any awkward episode. I never found out why she'd done it, what she'd had in mind. I always assumed that it had simply made sense to her not to be covered with anything so specific and small-minded as clothing, that she had wanted to be plain, unfrilled. That was the one way it seemed Ellie-like.

But look at her now. In her blouse and sweater, decently covered and nicely nourished, a slightly frumpy young blonde woman. You could walk down the street and see a billion people a lot weirder than Ellie. Look at her now. She was clearing the table—she never did this—she was scraping food from dishes and stacking them in the sink. "You don't have to do that," I said, but I was the world's most delighted hostess.

She said, "You made the dinner." She looked small and short-waisted and sweet, standing over the suds. She washed all the plates and the silverware and even scoured the pan in which a chicken had been cooked that she had eaten none of.

At the end she took the coffee cups and the wineglasses from the table, and one of the glasses broke in the sink. "It's okay," I said. "It's not crystal, it's just from the restaurant. Only get your hands out of the sink."

But Ellie wanted to gather up the pieces to throw them out. "No," I said. "Don't be a jerk." She fished several large pieces of broken glass up from the bottom, with her bare hands. "You jerk," I said, but there were no cuts on her, no swirls of blood in the water. She kept on washing the dishes, in that water full of glass shards, like someone swimming with sharks. Nothing happened. The dishes got clean.

"You worry too much," she said, and I was glad to believe she was right.

For a while after that I didn't see Ellie. She wouldn't come to visit. I talked to her on the phone, but Ellie wasn't good on the phone. When I mentioned her career in letter carrying, she changed the subject or she got sarcastic. She hedged about coming to dinner again. Whenever I wasn't around Ellie for a while, she got vaguer and harder to talk to. She wouldn't answer questions straight. Okay, I thought, you don't want to tell me, I don't want to know. I did get incurious after a point; Ellie could tell. If I didn't see Ellie for weeks at a time, the world around me—the street, the restaurant, the daily speech of friends—was clearer. As an idea held in the mind—a coherence of thought—the world was easier to formulate without Ellie.

Toward the end of spring, Doug's bar suddenly got very popular—who knew why? Certain people found their way there and others followed, and the nights there were denser, heavier with the shifting presence of people. They were good-looking, as a group, with nervy haircuts and effective clothes. When the hot weather came, there was the din of the air conditioners and the compression of those bodies in the room drinking, eating, talking, looking for trouble.

Doug was happy. He rushed around behind the bar, he poured

shots from a high, dashing angle, he shook Bloody Marys over his shoulder. At home he was almost too much to take, so pleased with himself. He saw the triumph of the place as some example of personal merit—he knew how things worked, and of course now he liked to tell me what he knew. He was not this way at all by nature, and I sometimes found it poignant, this new assumption of craftiness. But the bar's raging success also made him nervous. If the night turned out slower than usual, he scolded the waitresses in a tense and condescending way, and he made too many trips into the kitchen, tasting things, looking to see whether the silverware was dirty when it came out of the dishwasher.

I didn't take the place as seriously as Doug did. (Its name was Blue's, after a cat he had once owned.) To Doug the restaurant and its run on the site were historic, its nights part of the record of Manhattan social habits. I didn't think that at my age—I was in my thirties—I could be expected not to notice that life was large and various and that there were thousands of restaurants flashing on and off from year to year, billions of Blue'ses in the firmament.

Sometimes Doug didn't like the way I managed the floor. Oh, I put dowdy-looking people in the front, where they were the first ones seen from the street; I gave a party of nine to the slowest waitress; I let people linger too long at tables when there was a line waiting. Doug would corner me in an alcove, supposedly out of hearing of the rest of the help, and mutter at me (everyone knew). Usually I tried to calm him down, to point out how fine everything was going just as it was. He liked being calmed, if he wasn't too far gone. For a restaurant owner he was not awful. But I minded being muttered at in public, at the time and afterward.

In the hottest part of August, the place did a funny kind of erratic business, long dead times followed by streams of customers arriving.

It threw everyone's rhythm off. And peak hour was late, close to one; people didn't want to go back outside. They liked it better at Blue's. Outside the air in the streets was thick and buzzing. Bums screamed on corners, or they lay in doorways and writhed in their sleep. On the side streets kids went by with sticks, smashing car windows, shouting.

Once, at four-thirty in the morning, coming home from work, I saw a hooker on Second Avenue who looked like Ellie. She had the same round face under the makeup, the same kind of brushy blonde hair, and she was trying to stop cars. It wasn't Ellie. It wasn't even a woman, as it turned out. Ha, I thought, fooled me. I felt bad at having made the mistake—Ellie wouldn't do that, not that. But still there had been that terrible thrill of certainty: oh, no, now this.

One of the bartenders said that all the restaurants around us were having trouble with differents kinds of maniacs coming in. "New kinds?" I said. On certain nights everyone looked extreme to me—young girls with rings stuck through their lower lips, bearded fat men in T-shirts, boys in loud bermuda shorts.

Tom the bartender said that Jay from Ground Zero around the corner had had to stop two fights in one night. But the Ground always had more trouble; they were not as upscale as Blue's and not as good at stopping things before they happened.

Doug was better at keeping a lid on. For one thing, he was funny. His bar was a fairly good-humored place to sit; he told stories about the cats in the basement, he made up drinks with stupid names. Sometimes he would get sharp suddenly and say, "You're being an asshole," and usually, to my amazement, people shut up. Their man Doug, with his sly eyes and his floppy cowlick—was he speaking to them? It startled them to see him harsh. In truth, I admired Doug.

One night our ice machine broke just after eleven o'clock. Tom kicked it many times, first to get it to go and then to punish it. The busboy was sent to get sacks of ice from the bodega down the block. A few people were given tepid mixed drinks and not charged. They got drunker and complained anyway. Among them were two men who were telling stories about ice as a sexual tool, how they had touched this or that part of a woman with ice as long as she could stand it, longer. I didn't, after a few minutes, believe them—there was too much unanimity in the stories and the details, especially the physical ones, rang false—but their talk made my blood run cold; those were the words. There was in it such a desire to hold someone captive and to taunt nakedness, as though sex were a kind of bodily mockery. They talked as if this were ordinary, a simple boyish want.

Around two o'clock Ellie walked in. I couldn't believe at first that it was Ellie; she never came to Blue's. She had on a black sweatshirt—how could she stand it in this weather?—and an old Indian-print skirt. She looked oily and hot. Doug was waving to her from the bar, and she gave him a salute, her hand at her forehead. "Look who's here!" I said. I was so happy, so flattered, that she had come on her own like this. She pushed her way through the crowd at the front. But she didn't come to me, she went to Doug.

Maybe she wanted a drink right away. Too bad if she wanted anything with a lot of ice cubes. "Look who's here!" I said again, when I got near her. When we hugged, Ellie smelled pretty rank. "Are you hungry?" I said. "The cook is gone, but I could get you something cold."

Ellie thought this was funny. "Eat, eat," she said. She pinched my cheek, quite hard. "Too skinny."

Doug said we were honored by her visit. "I know," Ellie said.

Doug said, "What's your fancy?" meaning what did she want to drink, but Ellie was already straying to the other end of the bar. It was a long bar, and she walked jiggling in time to the music on the jukebox.

"Restless tonight," I said, as if Doug needed to be told. Ellie stood, twitching on the beat. I watched a man talk to her; Ellie made a face—she stretched her lips back like a dog baring its teeth or a child imitating a monster. I thought this was to scare the man away, but he kept talking to Ellie. They had a conversation for several minutes, Ellie still jiggling, and the man bought a glass of beer for her from Tom. Ellie walked away with it, and the man yelled out to her. "Young lady," he said. "Young *lady*." "What are you doing?" I said when she came back.

"Hey, don't mug the customers," Doug said.

"That's me," Ellie said. "The midnight mugger. Better call the cops right now." I hate it when she' s like this, I thought, although actually this was new, a new twist.

"I didn't know you drank beer," I said. Usually Ellie liked fussy, girlish drinks—Brandy Alexanders, Golden Dreams. Two cream drinks like that and she was snockered. She swallowed her beer now without saying anything. "You see your mother lately?" I said.

"Nope. Why, do you see her a lot?"

"Well, you know she calls me. I don't call her." I didn't have to disown Roslyn like that, although I really didn't like her much. "She always invites me to come visit her new house," I said. "It's a nice house, huh?"

"Beeyootiful. So nice it's criminal. Maybe you should call the cops on that house." Ellie was jiggling away from us again.

"What is this thing with the cops?" Doug said.

"Maybe she needs them here," I said.

Ellie was twirling now in the middle of the floor. She made fluttery motions with her hands toward the jukebox. A man who was very drunk started to dance with her. It was not dancing—neither of them was in rhythm—it was a horrible kind of flailing about. Ellie swept her hands around, touching the floor. She tossed her skirt up a few times and let out little yipping screams. "I can't stand it," I said. I was talking to myself, I saw—Doug had gone down the bar to serve someone. The man tried to weave in closer to Ellie. He put an arm around her—Ellie made the same grimace she had before, an extended snarl, and she bit his shoulder. The man yelled, he backed away, and then—to my great relief—he laughed. And then the song ended.

Another song came on at once, a slow number. Ellie was swaying. I had the idea to go over and try to lead her in a waltz. She let me guide me her a little, and then she swooped and almost fell on me. People started hooting and clapping, and I could barely move for embarrassment. But Tom had once danced a drunk out the door; I thought maybe I could lead Ellie to the back, sit her down. Ellie spun out of my grip and went up and sat on a barstool. I was stranded in the middle of the floor. "Great move," Doug said. "That helped a lot." Another drunk was dancing now. At the bar Ellie sat with her head in her hands.

The busboy brought a bin full of ice to the bar and had to skirt around the dancing drunk. Ellie glanced up and cackled at this. The busboy looked as if he wanted to sock her. She put her head down in her hands again. No one was going near her; maybe she would stay still, fall asleep. I thought she must be tired, from being like this for a while.

At the bar they were all clapping for the dancing drunk. "No dancing," Doug yelled. "Sit down, Baryshnikov. Come on." He sounded weak and pleading, I thought. Tom went over and pulled the plug on the jukebox, and there was a sudden cold silence; people groaned. When the man sat down, the jukebox went on again, to a different, softer song.

"Every weirdo nut freak is here tonight," Malcolm said to me.

Some people at one of the booths were signaling for their check, and I went to find their waitress. When I came back, Malcolm was shaking Ellie awake, as if he were a cop at Port Authority. Ellie could not have been out for long. "It's all right," I said. "I know her."

Ellie was quite awake now, and mad. She had hold of Tom's wrist, but I made her let go. "Do you feel all right?" I said.

"She feels fine," a man said. "Show her you're fine."

Ellie got up and ran the length of the bar and halfway back. She started out trotting like a little racehorse but on the return she was zigzagging, knocking into people on purpose. What I didn't like was the way she was laughing to herself. She's gone, I thought. To use those phrases—gone, over the edge, *out* there—made me sound to myself as if I knew something about it. I knew perhaps a little. But to watch Ellie now was to be humbled in that respect. Somebody pushed Ellie when she knocked into him. "Come back," I said. "Listen to me for a minute."

"Get her calmed down," Doug said.

Don't *tell* me, I thought, but I couldn't yell at him in his own bar. Ellie ran around to people lifting up her sweatshirt. Underneath there was bare skin—her breasts visible in flashes, pale and mauve-centered. Mostly people seemed stunned or bothered, but one man wanted to touch her. "Okay," I said. "It's time to go. I'll take you home."

Ellie really did look like another person by now—her face was closed and her mouth moved in nasty half-smiles. "I'm fine," she said. "I'm fine right here."

Ellie was at least safer here than she would be on the street. On the street she was an accident about to happen. This expression, as soon as I thought of it, rang in my ears like a song lyric. "Well, sit down then," I said. "Be good."

Ellie raised her sweatshirt and flashed her chest again. "Shit," Doug said.

"Okay," I said. "That's it. You have to go."

"Let's go, let's go," Ellie said, but she didn't move.

"Could I have my purse?" I said to Doug. He handed it to me from behind the bar. I said to Ellie, "You can stay at our place if you want." Otherwise I would have to stay at Ellie's with her. Ellie lived in a residence hotel—would they let a second person stay in her room? Of course; they wouldn't care, they'd never notice.

"I'm not ready yet," Ellie said.

"We could take a cab. I'm very tired, personally."

Ellie got up then. She seemed to like the idea of a cab. I took her arm—I wasn't sure this was the thing to do, but Ellie leaned on me, as though she were waiting to be helped. "See you later some time," I told Doug.

When we were out on the hot street, I felt triumphant at having managed this. "We'll just walk to the corner and we can get a cab right away," I said.

"I don't want to wait on that corner," Ellie said.

"How about the other side of the street?"

"It's the same *thing*," Ellie said.

"You want to wait right here? It'll take longer."

Ellie smiled her nasty half-smile. I felt stupid—here, there, what did it matter where we waited? Ellie was right to laugh. She was laughing now—that mean, soft cackle. She makes herself do it, I thought, she doesn't have to laugh like that. And no cabs were coming. An old bum wanted a quarter from us and wanted to tell us what lovely young girls we were; some teenage boys went by making kissy noises at us. Ellie was getting jumpy—she stood kicking at things in the gutter and then rocking back and forth on the curb.

"Okay," I said. "We'll walk west. Another block and a half, okay?" Ellie acted as if she hadn't heard. "Come on," I said. "I know you got comfortable in that spot, but we have to move on."

"Oh, for God's sake," Ellie said. "The bullshit you talk. I can't believe I have to listen."

There was a cab—I waved at it wildly, but it didn't stop.

"He had people," Ellie said. "Didn't you see?"

"I didn't see." I had Ellie walking now. We would find a cab on the Bowery, where there were always cabs.

"You never see anything. You're always thinking about something else."

We were on Second Street, walking past a chain-link fence in front of a dark, empty parking lot. Someone had stuck a woman's shoe—a red high-heeled sandal—on one of the fence posts. "Oh, God, look at that," Ellie said.

"That?" I said. I would have to call Ellie's mother in the morning. Ellie would hate that.

When we got to the Bowery, Ellie said, "This is too big a street. I can't stand on a street this big."

"Oh, just wait a second. You can wait a *second*."

Ellie stopped on the corner and flung her hands out in front, as if she were measuring the street or ordering it to stop. The Bowery, with its long highway-like dividers, was starkly lit and relatively quiet at this hour. I wondered if it looked larger or smaller to Ellie with less traffic on it. Ellie turned then and ran—but she didn't run away from the Bowery, she ran along it, heading uptown. I saw her back, the Indian skirt streaming behind her, her elbows bent in the lumpy black sweatshirt. I yelled her name; I scolded her to come back. People on the street were quite excited by this; some of them yelled with me. "Ellie," they called in falsettos, "ELLEEE." Somebody shouted, "Well, go get her, girl. Don't stand there," but I had already resolved not to run. I was to remember this very clearly after, that I had decided not to run. It was true that within less than a minute I couldn't see Ellie anymore—she was going so fast she was already out of sight, or she had ducked into a deli or another bar or a gas station or a flophouse—but I had decided before then.

Let Ellie get home by herself; everyone else did. I thought of an entire city of people walking up their own stairs, letting themselves in with their own keys. Secretly I applauded the city for this, that it required people not to be fragile or foolish. How come Ellie deserved special help just to get home? I was indignant on behalf of myself—now of course I lived with Doug, but all the years before—the threats on the street, the gas leak in the kitchen, the man on the fire escape. Who did Ellie think she was?

Ellie had been nasty and insulting, not just now but in the past too. She had called me a coward, she had jeered at my way of speaking, she had tried to talk my mother into burning some clothes of mine, she had told Doug he was a poison and he knew it. It struck me, with some spite, that Ellie was right to say I was always thinking of something else. All through the panic of seeing Ellie crazy I was thinking of how I wanted to get home myself, how I was tired, sick of people. My own bed, a book, an apple, and a glass of cold milk. I wanted Ellie to disappear; I was glad when I couldn't see Ellie anymore.

Ellie would be fine; her craziness would protect her. She didn't live all that far away; her hotel was in the Twenties, perfectly walkable. I thought of the theory that if any would-be muggers come near you the safest thing is to talk to yourself like a crazy person—that scares them away. Ellie would be fine; what was fine anyway?

And perhaps it would do no good to run after Ellie because Ellie wasn't even running any more. Maybe she was stopped somewhere. I knew I could go into the deli, the bar, the gas station, and the flophouses to look for Ellie, of course. I didn't want to go into any of them—who would? Who wanted to see the beat-up old men and the young ones with prison haircuts in the flophouse lobby, the leering guys at the gas station, the leftover drunks at the bar, even the bums at the deli? I was afraid of them. Still I might have done it, for Ellie.

When I got home, I waited half an hour and then I got out of bed and called Ellie. There was no answer in her hotel room. Ellie had her own phone; she was pretty much a permanent resident there. The other tenants could probably hear the ringing; I felt a little bad about letting it ring for such a long time. I tried again later, and then twice later when Doug got home. "She's out wandering," Doug said. He said this as a kind of sober fact, not reassuring but tolerable. He put his arm around me when he spoke.

I watched Doug undress, and then I fell asleep. In my sleep I phoned many times. Once Ellie said she was on an island under the ocean, and once a creature answered the phone and hissed like a snake. I woke at seven and started calling again. I got used to the particular ringing sound the phone made, sharp with a lot of vibration in it. Each time I called, it seemed more certain the ringing wouldn't stop until I hung up.

In the kitchen, yesterday's newspapers, in a mess on the table, were full of the usual stories of children falling from windows, men going berserk and stabbing their families, buildings tumbling on passers-by. I had glanced at these stories all my life and never thought of them as true exactly, not lies but not part of the fabric of life for most people. If I worried about muggings, car accidents, and bridge collapses, my experience generally was of these things not happening—the boys walking toward me crossed the street, the car in the oncoming lane slowed down, the bridge rattled but didn't give way. In the nature of things, I expected, more or less, that if I waited long enough, Ellie would have to come in and answer the phone.

II.

Doug and I called Ellie's hotel all morning. We made the manager open the room—she wasn't there—and we kept leaving messages anyway. I thought about going over in person but then I talked myself out of it. When our phone rang in the afternoon, I thought it must be Ellie. It was my mother, speaking in a very low, even voice. The police had just called the house, she said. For Stanley. She said other things, before she got to the heart of the matter, but the word *police* blocked them out.

Ellie's body had been found in a parking lot. An attendant had found her when he came to open up in the morning; she had been stabbed, after what was probably a long beating and a bruising rape. Her clothes were thrown up a tree in another part of the lot. Her purse, with her empty wallet, was under a car. She'd been dead for a few hours.

When my mother first told me, I wept and I said it was my fault and I told her and everyone else all the details of the night before. Everyone was kind to me, no one said anything to blame me, and no one needed to hear me go on. Something tremendous had happened, and my own deliberations, my agonies of regret, were not of consequence any more, and were bothersome to everyone.

Doug and I took a train to Westchester, to Ellie's mother's house, where everyone was gathering. The house was full of relatives, and my stepfather was in a big leather armchair, with people milling around him. My mother was sitting next to him, holding his hand. He was all jowls and fierce eyes, like a sick animal. He said, "Hello, hey there," when he saw me. Later, Doug offered him a cigarette, and when Stanley exhaled, he made a slow sighing noise as if his breath were giving out. As if he had been waiting all night to make that thin, defeated hiss.

In the weeks right after Ellie's death, I didn't care if I was seen crying on the street. I would be walking with Doug or with a friend on some crowded block, and as we talked I would feel my face turn into a weeping face. I was beyond anything like ordinary constraint, I was above having any feeling at all about who saw me do what. There was something exalted in this, and I wanted to hold on to this larger view, this larger freedom, but it passed when the first extremities of grief passed, and the smallness of life came back.

I left Doug, or we left each other, within that year. He was very nice to me right after Ellie died, and I was glad of his comfort. But I didn't want to be in Blue's anymore, and I didn't like to hear Doug talk about it, and he was attached to the place, so we never got over that rift. It wasn't Blue's or anyone who'd been in Blue's who killed Ellie; I didn't think that.

The police, who had other opinions, made several visits to Blue's, asking Doug and Malcolm questions. Malcolm also thought that undercover cops were turning up at the bar for a while, and he was probably right. I never believed they would catch anyone. I thought Ellie's death was something beyond solution; I didn't think its horror could be puzzled out or unsealed.

I'd spent years in Blue's, first as a waitress and then as Doug's helpmeet, and even though I couldn't stand to go in there anymore, Blue's was hard to leave. I'd been at home there, coolly contented with what I thought I knew; all that snappy assurance that Ellie hated had been a great pleasure to me.

Leaving Doug gave me something to do. For a long time I was quite pumped up about my decision. My friends got to hear me talk about it, instead of about Ellie. And I started to think about Ellie less. All the same, hardly a day passed when I didn't beg for a revision in time, when I didn't scheme to run down the block after Ellie.

There are mistakes that can't be fixed. Doug said that to me once, and he was not even talking about Ellie, he was talking about things we had done and said to each other. As a proverb—and it did settle in my mind as one—it had a pleasing stubbornness, a lucid finality. It was a wall to rest against.

III.

ON THE OTHER HAND, Ellie's parents, separately and together, could not get over feeling that they should do something. Something had to be done; they were tortured and bedeviled and lit up by the dream of doing something. Roslyn, Ellie's mother, called the police station at all hours of day and night. She thought of new facts that might serve as leads, she threatened the police with lawsuits for not working hard enough. She got me to call them too—I couldn't refuse Roslyn anything—and once she actually got me to go down to the precinct house and try to sweet-talk a detective into putting more men on the case. I made a fool of myself, but I did it.

Stanley, my stepfather, got caught up in the idea of suing. It seemed so satisfying to him, that someone might award the family money because they'd suffered wrongly. He was the owner of a shoe company, plagued by new risks every season, and hard sums meant a lot to him. He wanted to sue the police, he wanted to sue Blue's for having served Ellie alcohol, he wanted to sue the psychiatrist who had seen Ellie last. He did consult lawyers, and they might have taken his money to carry any one of these complaints to court, but the legal wheels turned so slowly, that this became another vexation of his life, and he washed his hands of the lawyers in outrage.

I never argued with either Stanley or Roslyn, and they wouldn't have paid any attention if I had. They were busy tiring themselves out and were perhaps moving closer to the peace that comes from exhausting all possibilities. Neither of them blamed me—never that I heard, anyway—but they liked to get me going in their schemes, and they knew I would go. The three of us had become our own little version of a family, who mourned by running around in circles; this was somewhat hard on my mother. Ellie's brother, who might've cared, didn't.

I was nicer to Roslyn than I'd ever been; I was nicer to most people. I had become more vigilant, more attentive. What was the point of all my remorse if not that? It was one of my few consolations, to think I had been instructed and improved. I was ready for the next time, for the next test; in fact, I was waiting for it eagerly. For a long time I really was very careful.

I was working then for a friend's business renting houseplants to offices (I had done the books at Blue's), and in the closeted tensions of a tiny company I was famous for my good temper with nutty clients and balky coworkers. Everyday peskiness was easy for me. In the leafy footage of our showroom, I was kind to fools and tyrants without thinking about it.

Roslyn started to call me more often. She needed to know: Did Ellie ever live with her boyfriend in college? What did Ellie say about her father? Did Ellie eat too many sweets and could that have sent her over the top mentally? Did I think she and Ellie looked a lot alike? Very similar, right? What if Roslyn herself, in the flesh, went into Blue's some night and the killer was still hanging out there—wouldn't he be spooked if he saw her, and then she could tell who he was? She was excited about this last idea.

"And then what?" I said. "You would arrest him then? Half of Blue's is spooked all the time anyway. What are you talking about?"

"I thought you would help me," Roslyn said. "I thought you would be better about this. You think I'm an idiot."

"Sometimes you are," I said. "Not really, but, you know."

But Roslyn wouldn't let me take it back. And after this, when Roslyn left her messages on the phone machine, I waited days to call her back or I forgot altogether. Once she cried on the tape and I didn't pay much attention, as if she had been some person on the street, another stricken stranger I walked right by.

So bit by bit I got less careful altogether. I was rude to my mother when she asked me nosy questions. I didn't visit a friend who was sick. I wasn't terrible, but I was neglectful. Things distracted me, and I stopped being afraid of the consequences. I came to think that, if Ellie came back, I would be the same as I was; I would lose patience with her all over again. Maybe.

One night Doug called to tell me that Roslyn had, after all, paid a visit to Blue's. "She's put on a lot of weight, hasn't she?" he said. "But she looks okay, I guess. She sat at the bar for a while."

"How'd she act?"

"Cheerful and chatty, at first. There were men who talked to her, and she seemed happy about that. And then I think people were getting obnoxious—you know what this place can be like—they were teasing her and sort of baiting her. She got upset. In the end I went out and got her a cab myself, because she was scared to walk to the lot where she'd left her car, which was maybe four blocks away."

So Roslyn had spooked herself. I thanked Doug for taking care of her, or doing whatever he did.

"You could come back too," he said. "For a drink, I mean. You don't come in anymore." After we split up, Doug and I used to go on dates, or I would stroll into Blue's and we'd have a little light sprightly talk across the bar. We almost got back together often. We were done with that now; we were on to other things. "Oh, I'll turn up some time," I said, and then I made some joke about how he shouldn't water the drinks that night; it was the kind of thing my stepfather used to say to him. Stanley would say, "Those crazy East Village customers still breaking all the glasses?" "The customers are behaving themselves," Doug would say. "I'm the one that makes trouble." He was a good sport like that with me now; we were down to sportsmanship.

I did phone Roslyn to find out how she was. "I'm not doing that again," she said. "You were right." I was? Sometimes Roslyn surprised me.

Roslyn had, yes, had an intuition that the killer was somewhere in the bar, but this had not been a triumphant sensation but a terrifying one. I might have told her. For a long time after Ellie was killed, people used to ask me whether I wasn't afraid to walk around at night. "Yes," I said, "sure," but I couldn't stay inside every night, could I? And often when I was walking around in my own neighborhood, which was, after all, the neighborhood where it had happened, I would pass some person on the street, and a chill would go straight through me. A shudder of recognition, but fleeting. I would see men with scars on their necks and pointed teeth, men with shaved skulls and one ear gone, men with hawkish gazes and dead mouths.

Demons' faces. Who knew what they really were? I remembered thinking: I'm out of my depth.

"Blue's is something," Roslyn said. "Why did you let Ellie come into Blue's?"

"It wasn't my idea."

"I didn't even want her to live in New York," Roslyn said. "I opposed it. You know what she was like. Talk to her and talk to the wall. I argued till I was purple. Didn't matter."

"She was a stubborn one," I said.

Even now, I rarely thought of Ellie without arguing with her memory. There were little bright spots of indignation in my missing Ellie. All that insistence on sticking to her own methods, on not going along with what she didn't believe in. She got mad when you tried to tell her about anything. And look at her now; this whole year, I'd wanted to say to her, *See, I was right.*

Imagine being Ellie and being told you were wrong about everything; the sky wasn't the same blue you saw it as. It took determination to go on being Ellie—blocked at every turn and still running around defiant. That last run down the street had of course been a continuation of her argument with me, her argument with the world.

"She was such a pill sometimes," I said.

"Oh, well," Roslyn said. "Nothing we can do about it now, is there?"

Roslyn had her amazing moments.

"You okay?" she said. "Still there?"

But I did wonder: What's next, when Roslyn gets her wind back? Will she start digging up the body, scolding the cemetery staff for not burying it neatly enough?

"I have to tell you, you worry too much," Roslyn said. "That's your whole problem."

Stanley called later to find out if Roslyn was all right. He had heard the story. He said, "That part of town is not for her, I told her." He went on a little about how Blue's *could* be liable for serving Ellie if she'd been intoxicated when she'd come in, but I could see he was winding down too. From repeating themselves over and over, he and Roslyn were reaching an ending to this year. They were coming to the point where they'd had enough.

ON THE ONE-YEAR ANNIVERSARY of Ellie's death, we all went to Roslyn's house for a private gathering. There was a table with photographs of Ellie on it. In one of them, Ellie at fifteen had her hair in rows of tiny braids, with bits of hardware I had stuck in them, and she was giggling (there she was; oh, look at that face). People stood around with coffee and cake, talking about current events and interior decor. Mozart was playing on the stereo. Ellie's brother put a piece of chocolate cake in front of Ellie's picture, but that was as ceremonial as it got.

"This was a lovely idea," everyone said as they left, and actually it wasn't bad.

I told my friends, whew, I can't believe it, my hysterical family is calming down. I made fun of Roslyn's panic in the bar, and I did a fair imitation of Stanley's gruff attempts at speaking legalese. My friends laughed, as they were supposed to do, and they said, now everything will be normal, you look great, you can get back on track in your old life. What? I said. What? They were confident about my prospects and their own. They were looking ahead, and they wished me well. I felt like someone talking to them across a great divide.

Ragazzi

"Have you considered going and soaking your head?" Noelle says. "Have you thought about playing in traffic?" Damian, her friend's nineteen-year-old son, has just asked if she knows she's reading the only newspaper in the house.

"You're too old to read anyway," Damian says. "Look at how you're squinting at the page."

She's trying to read the *Herald Tribune*, the one English-language paper on sale here. Jennifer, Damian's mother, must've gotten up earlier and bought it. It's a skinny paper that doesn't divide up into sections. "My, my, this is interesting," Noelle says. "I might have to read it twice." Damian tilts his head under the paper to look at the back page; he is just about lying in Noelle's plate.

Noelle doesn't really like to read the paper when she's on vacation anyway. She's been in Italy only for a week, but the President looks like someone dimly familiar from a long time ago.

She can't believe he's still carrying on. All the same, she reads a few paragraphs about his tax proposals, slowly, before she gives the paper to Damian.

Damian is a cute-looking boy—he has blondish hair in tight sheep-curls and dark, starry eyes; he resembles his mother. He's been in trouble this year, of a particularly stupid kind. He and some friends of his were tossed out of school for spray-painting graffiti in the dorm—they drew swastikas and wrote WHITE POWER and BACK TO AFRICA all over the study lounge. Also DIE, DYKES. Pretty primitive stuff.

Damian is not a brainless oaf. No one at his school is that neanderthal, his mother says. It's an expensive, progressive school; they all have to write long papers, take courses with eccentric titles, bluff with a sophisticated vocabulary.

So why did Damian impersonate a fascist goon? He has to do something, his stepfather says; youth needs to rebel. Noelle thinks that's too simple. He was with friends, of course—they goaded each other on, formed their own appreciative audience. Noelle can imagine them. The shared, smirky expressions, the overdone hilarity, the giddiness in their eyes.

Noelle doesn't think she knows Damian that well, although she has seen him on and off since he was very little. For the first year of his life his mother used to carry him around in a shawl embroidered with sequins; Noelle remembers his downy head in the crook of that glittery sling. Jennifer could take him like that to bars or rock concerts. He was a good, quiet baby. He's quiet still—or not talkative—but when he speaks, his voice is sharp and harsh. He says, "What?" all the time, in a hostile way Noelle has seen other teenagers use. It's possible, too, that he lost some hearing in those concerts of his babyhood. Maybe *what* is a real question.

Steve, Damian's father, played bass in a rock group that did a lot of touring. He's been out of Jennifer's life for years. The last time anyone saw him, he owned two failing nightclubs and he was stout and talked too much. Noelle herself lived with Bud, the lead singer of the band, for a while. That's how she and Jennifer know each other. Bud (to whom she was actually married at one point) died of an overdose when he was twenty-eight. He was in his prime, such as it was, and he remains forever in his glory days to people like Damian, who has been very interested in him lately.

Quiet as Damian is, he will ask anything. Yesterday he wanted to know if his mother had ever slept with Bud. And if either his mother or Noelle ever slept with more than one man at a time, or a man and a woman at the same time. Noelle doesn't answer these questions, which would only lead to more questions. Where would they end? "Forget it," she said. "I'm not talking. It's all buried in the sands of time."

Damian offered to tell her stuff about himself in exchange. "Ask me anything," he said. It was an offer with some appeal; he's not dumb. What he doesn't know is that Noelle is curious only up to a point. Nineteen is a good age, but she knows something about it already.

You can tell from a minute with Damian that he thinks of himself as enviable. He rubs his own arms as he looks at the newspaper; he nods and grunts at what he reads, as though the print were waiting for his response. He walks around half-dressed—at the moment he's wearing jockey briefs and thong sandals, a man with nothing to hide.

"So what are you girls doing today?" he says.

"We're checking out some churches," Noelle says. "Walking around." She isn't done with her morning coffee yet.

"Don't tire yourselves out."

They're in a small provincial city on the edge of Tuscany. This was Jennifer's idea, to rent a house in a beautiful setting and keep

Damian away from trouble for a while. There isn't much that he can do in the town. He can walk through the stone streets, hang out on a bench by the Duomo, stare at people from a cafe table. He doesn't speak Italian so he can't talk to the local youth, although some of them know what Jennifer calls MTV-English. Noelle has heard them call out, "What is happening? Oh, yeah," when they pass Damian on their mopeds, and Damian calls back, "Watch out, bros."

Noelle is only visiting for a few weeks—she doesn't have the whole summer with Damian, as his mother does—but she worries about his getting bored and restless. His stepfather won't be here till August.

At the moment Damian is saying, "Later for churches," not that Noelle blames him.

"What will you do then?"

"I'll trash the house and then go find some small children to beat up," he says.

"What a kidder you are," Noelle says.

Damian gives her a wicked smile.

Noelle wants to think he's not a bad kid. But he might be. It will be hard to tell about him for a while. "Try to keep away from the spray paint," Noelle says.

"Yeah, yeah."

"That was stupid shit, you know." Noelle happens to be married to a black man, for one thing. Did Damian think she wasn't going to say anything?

"What?" Damian says.

"Really stupid," Noelle says, and gets out of the kitchen. Enough said, discussion closed.

She has learned a few tactics from her job. She and her husband run a program teaching phys ed (gymnastics and drill teams and just plain hopping around) to kids in city shelters. Those kids—Noelle deals with the girls—have kept her on her toes.

Jennifer always says, "I don't know how you do it," a comment Noelle hates, since it sounds more like pity than admiration. In fact, Noelle worked with a ninth-grader this year who reminded her so much of Jennifer that she kept calling her Jen. The girl, whose real name is LaKeesha, was shy but nervy, a wild gymnast with a funny, blurting rhythm of attack.

Jennifer as a younger person always moved in sudden lurches. Bud called her Wired Simon, Simon being her last name. People had labels like that then—there was a girl everyone called Amy Nitrate and another who was only known as Felony.

Backstage Jennifer used to dance—silently, with herself—while the band played. Tiny jerks and jumps and grindings. Noelle, standing next to her, never knew whether she was supposed to watch or not. But she was proud too of Jennifer's purposefulness, her busy oblivion.

They spent a lot of time waiting in those days. They waited till the band got out of rehearsal, till the band was ready to eat. She and Jennifer had little projects for those moments—embroidering cowboy shirts, stringing beads. Noelle can't imagine herself ever being so placid. Now she hates being stuck anywhere; she likes her job because it keeps her running.

When Noelle talks to her husband on the phone from Italy, she tells him that the town is very beautiful. It has winding narrow streets, it has a church with amazing carvings on the front and a sweet-faced angel on top, it has a Roman amphitheater that is now a round street lined with shops. But she couldn't live here, she says, not her. It's an old place, and there's only one way of doing things here, no matter what the kids pretend. Growing up is probably easier here though, because you wouldn't have to learn everything the hard way. She has quite a gush of thoughts. "Anything else?" Lester says, nicely. He is glad she's not *too* happy, away from him, and then they say a few jokey sexy things to each other, which Noelle hopes Damian is not listening to in the other room.

THE TOWN IS SUNNY AND BUSY in the late morning, when Noelle and Jennifer go out on their walk. The buildings are sand-colored, with green shutters and tiled roofs. They have both picked out the houses they would buy if they ever moved here.

"Look at that," Jennifer says. A group of small boys is playing soccer in the square in front of a church. The boys dart around, yelling—Jennifer is proud of them, proud of everything in her town—but a passing tourist almost gets beaned by a flying ball.

"It's rough out here today," Noelle says.

The tourist, a man in a velour jogging outfit, glowers at the kids. "Probably would've done him good to get bipped on the head," Jennifer says. Noelle's kids at the shelter go around saying things like that: I'll whup you upside the head. They overdo the drawl—none of them really sounds that country—it's a kidding threat, usually. Some days it has seemed to Noelle that the kids, her kids, get hit on the head every minute of their lives; their heads are like punching bags, their heads are like the cranium around the brains of Muhammad Ali. Her kids make her dizzy; they live in a maze.

Jennifer came one day to help at one of the shelters, and actually she was good. She taught the little ones some ballet steps (she used to study ballet). Run hop skip leap. She had them moving so fast they didn't have time to talk back. *Tour jeter*, she told them, means throw yourself around.

Jennifer is saying something now about Damian but Noelle can't hear her because a bunch of mopeds is going past them; these streets are not as quiet as you would think. "To move here," Jennifer says. "He wants to move here instead of going back to school."

"What?" Noelle says.

Neither of them has ever seen Damian leave the house without complaining. What is going on here? Is he selling dope to the locals? Is he sleeping with the mayor's daughter? Or does he just really, really not want to go back to school?

"He decided he wants to spend six months reading science fiction and listening to African drum music," Jennifer says.

"Bud did that. I told Damian that."

For a moment they are both appalled at the lack of originality involved in being a certain age. "I thought he didn't like Africans," Noelle says.

Jennifer is embarrassed; this part embarrasses her. "He doesn't mean anything yet," she says.

But when will he, what counts? She and Jen let themselves slide a long time too, but nobody's leeway goes on forever. Things tighten up. Bud is the bad example.

"You know what else?" Jennifer says. "Damian wants to bring his girlfriend. Here. All next year."

Damian has talked to his girlfriend often this summer, at transatlantic rates. He has opinions and insights he wants her to hear. At times he has to repeat himself. They can tell she backs down when he gets hardheaded.

What will the two of them do here? Will Damian's stepfather pay for the girl too? Noelle thinks Damian gets too much money already, but no one has asked her, have they?

Damian has sworn, Jennifer says, that he'll get a job in a restaurant.

He'll learn Italian; he is learning already, from a tape. What the girl will do, he hasn't said. The girl is probably very excited. Who would know better than Noelle and Jennifer?

Jennifer says, "He'll see the town walls with snow on them," and her face, with its surrounding thistle of straw-tinted hair, is happy. She loves the idea of him here. The town walls, which are five hundred years old, are mounded over with dirt and grass, and you can walk on top of the ramparts and look down at the town. This is Jennifer's favorite walk at the end of the day.

"What if he gets too civilized?" Noelle says. "What if he starts sniffing the corks of wine bottles and kissing people's hands?"

"What if he becomes devoted to his beloved mother?" Jennifer says. "What if he throws himself at my feet and begs forgiveness for his filial terribleness?"

They are discussing how Jennifer will behave (icy but gracious) and what penance she will demand (his salary for the rest of his life) when they go into their favorite cafe. Noelle is deciding which little sandwiches to have when the place is suddenly invaded by a group of Italian kids a few years younger than Damian. They keep arriving—there must be fifteen or twenty of them—and they settle into tables with a lot of jumping around and calling back and forth. They are very lively and loud, males and females both. They cluster at a few tables, all talking at once. Every so often there is a groundswell of hilarity that travels fast. "It's like eating with a flock of seagulls," Jennifer says.

When the waiter comes, he can't hear Jennifer when she gives their order. "*Ragazzi*," the waiter complains. Noelle has heard a harassed schoolteacher calling this out to her class in a museum—*Ragazzi*! Boys and girls! The waiter rolls his eyes and lifts his hands as if he were vexed to pieces but in fact he isn't. They are quite harmless—not badly behaved really—and nobody minds noise here.

More of them are arriving. Two boys in jeans are pulling up chairs, crowding in. One of them—Noelle sees when she looks again—is Damian. What's astounding is that in this grouping he looks Italian. He looks smoother, droller, more sweetly vain.

Damian sees them. He says, "Hi, Mom," in a goofy voice and waves. The boy next to Damian says, "Hello, the mother of Damiano." He stands up, and the other boys stand up too. Are they making fun of Jennifer? They walk over to Jennifer's table (Damian too), and Damian's friend says their names—Marco, Pierluigi, Gianni, Giovanni, Luca—and they shake hands with Jennifer and Noelle. The girls are introduced from across the room—Paola, Ada, Elisabetta, and so on—and the girls wave from their seats.

Jennifer looks stupefied. When the boys go back to their table, she says, "Where is the American meathead we used to know as my son?" Noelle's husband has said that those episodes like Damian's graffiti are the tantrums of a generation of males whose dominion is passing away. Maybe the boys here are better, Noelle thinks, only because they have nothing to fluster them. No encroachments. Look how poised they are, how unnervous.

When she and Jennifer leave the cafe, Damian says, "*A più tardi*, Mom."

Noelle and Jennifer can't get over it. How did he hook up with these kids? Does the one boy translate for him? But they can't ask Damian because he's gone all day and not back for dinner, not back after midnight. "Go to bed," Noelle tells Jennifer. "Think: son, what son?"

In the small hours of the morning, there's a loud noise outside like an animal roaring. It's not an animal, it's a motorcycle. It zooms into their yard and stops. Noelle doesn't get out of bed, but she hears Jennifer talking. To Damian, who sounds slurred and drunk and quiet.

THE NEXT DAY NOELLE HEARS that Damian has bought this motorcycle from one of the boys—it's a big, nasty-looking bike, not one of those little mopeds. He spends every minute driving it all over, without a license and without a helmet. Driving crazy, even by Italian standards. He almost hits an old lady and he grazes somebody's cat, according to his own report.

He'll kill himself or someone else, Jennifer says; he's too much of a hot dog to be on a machine that powerful. She would stop him if she could. Noelle tries to remind her how many jerks in the world ride motorcycles and nothing happens to them. It's a weak argument. Damian uses it too.

Noelle tries to talk to him. She thinks they have a good rapport. "Hey, Damian," she says. "What the fuck are you doing?"

"What?" he says.

"Does the word *death* mean anything to you?" She says this in a kidding way, but it comes out pretty leaden; she startles herself.

"Don't panic," he says.

"It's not me you should be calming down," Noelle says. "It's your poor mother, for Christ's sake."

"If you told her I was a great driver," Damian says, "think she would buy that? You could try, it might work."

Noelle can't figure out how she's gotten herself in collusion against Jennifer.

"Want to go for a ride?" Damian asks.

And she's never liked motorcycles that much—too much wind in your face. On a country road they can be nice though.

"I bet you want to go," Damian says. "You need some excitement.

That's what you need, I can tell. Believe me." He is flirting with her and mocking her at the same time, a style she has never liked.

"I'm not going," she says.

"Think about it. Let me know."

Noelle is glad she never has to work with boys at the shelters. What would her husband say to Damian? Not for the first time, she misses Lester badly.

When Noelle talks to Lester over the phone, she tells him that she and Jennifer are leaving Damian alone. They're done with arguing. Damian's gotten testy in ordinary conversation, and they just keep away, not that they're afraid of him. "Why would you be afraid of him?" Lester says.

Noelle is ashamed before Lester, because she knows that they are afraid of Damian, she and Jennifer both.

It's a quiet time at the house, with Damian off tearing up the countryside. Jennifer says she can't lock him up, can she? She and Noelle have their routines, their morning walks, their visits to churches, their delicious lunches, their gelato snacks. In the afternoons, the town closes down. Corrugated aluminum shutters slide down over the store windows; it's like New York at night.

In the courtyard at home, Noelle leads Jennifer in exercises. The brick tiles get hot at this time of day and have to be covered with towels. Jennifer can't do sit-ups, because she still has back trouble from the time she fell off some bleachers, stoned, twenty-odd years ago. Noelle remembers Bud making funny remarks about it, your flying girlfriend. Her bad timing, her lack of forethought—Bud held these up to Noelle as familiar evidence, no surprise to him. "None of you know how to sit right," he said also. Bud was a confident person at this stage in his life, which made him better-looking than he would have been otherwise. And he was a glib talker; the first night, he told Noelle how much he liked to look at her breasts, to touch them, what a graceful shape they had; "I could even criticize them a little," he said.

Jennifer says that after her fall in the stadium her boyfriend Steve the bass player brought her a hyacinth macaw, not a cheap present. "They could be nice, those guys," Jennifer says. The band brought in some of their equipment and played for her in the hospital room, for about thirty seconds, until the nurses came in and stopped them. Doesn't Noelle remember the giant plant Bud dragged in one time, this huge tree?

They have had this conversation before, Noelle and Jennifer. Who was all right and who wasn't, why the two of them didn't know the difference then. Sometimes their prevailing ideas shift and they reapportion the blame.

Noelle tries to be fair about the past. She has known for a while that if Bud walked in right this minute—saying, *What? You thought I was dead?* the way people do in dreams—she wouldn't want to know him. She wouldn't have the patience for him now, even an older Bud. All the same her time with him was more or less sunny—heady and plenty informative—despite all the coarseness she now finds surprising. She tries to stay clear about all this; she tries to hold a balanced view.

Jennifer says that when she fell off the bleachers, she wished her boyfriend Steve could see her, doing something so zany. She thought it was the sort of funny accident you brag about, when she first started falling.

Could anyone be that dumb? they both say. But Noelle is tired of talking about the dumbness of youth. She wants to remember the smartness they had then and don't have now. She is sure she has lost certain kinds of understanding, and not just the wisdom of the appetites either.

One afternoon Damian comes back to the house with a group of Italian boys. They are shiny, cagey-looking boys, dapper and formidable. But they all live at home and will stay with their parents until they marry; even Damian has admitted this. They settle in the yard, around Damian's motorcycle, which has been giving him some trouble going uphill. The boys use a slapsticky pantomime to talk to Damian—they jump around, they make illustrative sound effects. Damian does his own awkward signaling (he looks like a break dancer, Jennifer says), or he punches the one friend to get him to interpret. The boys spend the afternoon cracking each other up. Maybe some of the laughing is forced, but still, Damian's part in this is amazing. From where Jennifer and Noelle are sitting in the yard, the group is like a cartoon of merry fellowship.

The boys do not, however, help him much with the motorcycle, and one afternoon Damian's bike stalls out as he's climbing the road to the top of the walls. Paola, one of the girls from town, is on the back of the bike. The bike slides into a ditch—the two of them scramble to get off it as it shimmies and falls, but Paola isn't fast enough and the bike lands on her foot. She has to wait, pinned like that and screaming, while Damian tries to lift the motorcycle off her. An old man comes along finally and helps him.

Jennifer hears this story when Damian calls from the local hospital. Damian is waiting while they take x-rays of Paola. He wants his mother to come pick him up.

On the car ride to the hospital, Jennifer keeps saying, "Why couldn't we stop him?" She asks this over and over in a number of ways. Poor Paola. What if the injury is worse than Damian says? And Jennifer is mad at whoever sold him the bike, mad at the boys of the town. "Some friends," she says. "Some pals."

The hospital is not a regular hospital at all, but a gray stone cloister. Only the sign with plastic lettering is modern. Damian is standing under the colonnades outside, and he looks miserable and sheepish, as he should. "She has a fracture," he says. Her family is here now, he wants to leave.

But Jennifer grabs Damian by the hand and takes him inside the building. Noelle can see from the portico that Jennifer is making him lead her to a group of Italians, a worried-looking bunch who must be Paola's family. What can Jennifer say to them? She doesn't even know much Italian. Something apologetic; they are all nodding gravely, one of them pats Jennifer's arm. Damian is looking at his shoes.

On the ride home Jennifer doesn't speak at all. It's Damian who tries to be the talky, social one. He says, "Do you believe they put sick people in a place that looks like a set from *The Addams Family*? The place is a joke."

Jennifer won't speak to him. Noelle helps him out; she talks about hospitals she has known. She can feel that Jennifer is angry at her for showing this much mercy to him. It's a long car ride.

Damian has some bruises on his face from the fall, and when they get him home, he lies out in the yard, as if the sun will help. He keeps this up for the next few days.

The bike, which was left on the trail, is stolen by the time someone goes back to look for it. Noelle thinks that Damian is probably relieved. Perhaps his friends know who has it, but they won't tell. He's still an outsider to them.

Paola has a cast on her foot and is healing well so far, but her parents don't want Damian coming around. Mostly Damian stays by himself in the courtyard, listening to music through his headphones. He has not been out in the town since the accident, and when the boys from town come to visit he's so quiet that they leave.

He lies on a rug on the brick tiles, with nothing on but his underpants. Noelle doesn't envy him. "Hey, Road Runner," she says, to wake him up. "Hey, little Hell's Angel." She has to say it over to make him hear.

"Let me ask you," he says, when he sits up. "Did Bud like Italy?"

"He was never here."

"Smart man."

Damian has different plans now for next year. He'll go back to his old school and transfer later. Right now he is starting to complain about how much longer the summer is. Six weeks, he is counting them, six.

Noelle thinks he will perk up again before the season is out. "Wait and see," she tells Jennifer. God knows what other phases he'll think up, but Noelle speaks to Jennifer in cheery, hopeful terms.

Noelle offers, of course, the example of themselves. Look how okay they turned out finally. (She avoids mentioning Bud here.) What they can't remember, Noelle notices, is how they learned not to be idiots. How could this be so lost to memory? No incidents or scenes, no tag-phrases from this stage, no special color to it at all.

But Noelle does remember something, from when Bud started shooting drugs, and she started too, every now and then. On a certain night, she doesn't remember passing out, but when she came to on the sofa, people were standing over her, looking scared. They had been trying to walk her around, to get her awake, for a while. "I'm fine," she said. It made her smile that all of them were so worried. Now she wonders how long they would have kept trying their home methods of resuscitation. Bud told her she should go outside and be out in the open air. It took the two of them a long time to find their coats, get their shoes on. Noelle felt great on the street, perfectly happy, but Bud threw up in the gutter. They were in London then, so at least no one they knew was walking by. Bud said, "I feel like a fool." This was so unlike him that it stopped her short, to hear him speak this way. *Listen to that*, she thought. *Can you believe that?* He surprised her, which is what she remembers.

Partners

When Nathan saw the reports of what Hurricane Andrew did to Homestead, he didn't go to the phone right away, but he thought of going. His friend Rae had been living in Homestead the last time he'd spoken to her, but that had been years ago, so who knew where she was now? Probably not there. Homestead was always a ratty town—where Rae lived was just a big settlement clustered around the highway. Motels did okay there, because it was one of the last stops before the main entrance to Everglades Park. Rae had managed the Hotel Caribe, known to her friends as the C'rab. (Nathan, actually, had started that joke.)

In the papers Nathan saw photos of houses in rubble and trees mowed down like grass. On TV he saw people getting army food and liking it; he watched families settle into tent cities. So finally he telephoned. The Caribe didn't have a working phone; probably it didn't have a roof anymore either. The Red Cross didn't know anything about the whereabouts of any Rae Davidson. The Public Health Service didn't have her on any list.

What could he do? Either she was fine or she wasn't; he gave up. But then after a few months had passed, he tried the Caribe again, and the phone rang and a woman answered. She said, "Well, you know what? I have to tell you, she doesn't work here any more. She moved out, smart girl. You didn't know that? She's working over by the travel agency at the mall."

And then Nathan found her right away, at home under new listings. When she answered the phone, her voice had gotten old and nasal. She sounded like one of Nathan's aunts. "Hello?" she said. "Hello?"

"Hey," Nathan said. "You didn't get blown to bits."

Rae yelped with surprise a few times. She seemed very perky and glad to hear from him. "Do you believe it?" she said. "Me in the middle of a hurricane, how typical."

"X-Rae," he said. "You ought to come back to New York, where it's safe."

"I was safe. I was down in the cellar of the motel, with the washing machines. I could feel the whole building getting slammed. All the glass was breaking—that dumb plywood didn't do a thing. My cat wouldn't leave the cellar for three days. You would like this cat."

"How's our couch?"

Someone overhearing them—Nathan's wife, for instance—might have thought they were ex-lovers, but they weren't, although the couch had been in three different houses they'd lived in together, and had been kept by Rae as a souvenir.

"It looks like hell," she said. "It got flooded and waterlogged. But it's still alive. I'm sitting on it at the moment."

The couch had been bought in a triumphant moment, when the

two of them were happy over a sudden increase in their cash flow. It was a long leather sofa, pale taupe in color, foolishly suave. The office furniture, they called it. The corporate suite.

That was when they were living in Miami together. Now Nathan was back in New York. Rae could've come back too if she'd wanted to. But you could never get her to understand that. And Florida probably suited her. Nathan had always thought that Rae was a little lazy, not driven enough for their partnership. But they had worked together well for a while, and they had been friends before that.

When they were living in New York, a long time before, they called each other every day. They walked places with their arms around each other. They used special nicknames; they bought each other presents. They told stories about one another to anyone who would listen. People were very sentimental about friendship then.

Nathan himself was skinny and gangling, but he liked his own style, the Santa beard and the jeans that were too short on him. He could see Rae wasn't attracted and he didn't pester her (except once, with bad results they both chose to forget). She seemed to regard him as someone who hadn't passed through puberty yet. Rae had a lot of romances that went on for a month or so, not longer. She was a ticket-taker in a rock club and there were a lot of men around.

She was seeing a drummer at the time she got hit by a bus. She had just left his place at noon when she crossed the street and a bus rounded the corner without slowing down. It knocked her sideways into the gutter, and her hip broke in the fall.

This was the end of Rae's ticket-taking, and the beginning of a long stay in Nathan's apartment. She was a good-tempered convalescent, happy to stay still and lie around watching TV. He made her weird suppers—scrambled eggs à la Nathan, with salami and soy sauce—which she ate with a nice show of enthusiasm. The two cats were always sleeping on the sofa with her. As she got better, she would hobble out to bars with him. "Here she is," Nathan would say. "She-devil with a crutch." "Our own Christmas Seal girl," their friend Tom would say. Toward the end Nathan got a little tired of her, and they had a fight about who paid more for groceries. And a woman named Judy was showing an interest in him. When Rae went back to her own place, he was relieved.

It was a year before Rae finally collected a big wad of insurance money, and she and Nathan began having talks about going into business together. Nathan had the idea first. He had been working as a carpenter on loft renovations and he was terrible at it—slow, sloppy, and confused; he had no idea what he was doing. "Hammer much?" Rae said, when she visited him at a job one time. "Is this a hammer?" Nathan said. On the side he started doing some low-level dope-dealing, on a very amateur basis, teeny-tiny amounts of cocaine. And the elation he felt at the sight of a profit made him bolder in his thinking.

It was a pretty, breezy spring day when Rae went to the bank to get the money out. Nathan waited outside with their friend Tom, who was serving as escort for the walk home. When Rae came out of the bank, she was red-faced and smiley, a tad too hilarious. She said the clerk had asked her if anyone was coercing her into this cash withdrawal. Was anyone making her do this against her will? What a joke.

Nathan looked at himself and Tom—two long-haired white guys in T-shirts—and wondered how they must have looked to someone inside. Two figures of incipient menace, with dark expressions and bored postures. While Rae was laughing it up, Nathan was letting this picture settle in him as a glimpse of the future, a hope for things to come.

The other thing Nathan liked to remember was being with Rae in a hotel in La Paz. Their room had a terrace and they would sit out there at night, in that godforsaken city, with all the sounds from the street coming up and the old buildings looking chalky and dead. Rae was scared then but she was giddy too, and she kept Nathan up all night talking. (They were not sleeping a lot then anyway.) They played a long game of Botticelli and they talked about what was safe to eat in Bolivia. Rae said the body was a mystery, wasn't it, and why did no one think of bones as the holy part, if that was the part that endured. What leisure they had then, to have thoughts without bearings, to have airy arguments. They liked their bone-talk; that was a happy night for them.

"So can a leather sofa be fixed?" Rae was saying over the phone. "You know more about sofas than I do."

Nathan had tried a lot of businesses, after he'd left off smuggling, but what he was finally good at, much to his own surprise, was buying and selling antique furniture. But he saw almost no sofas; upholstered furniture didn't last.

"How fixed do you want it?" Nathan said. He knew some tricks for quick patch-ups. He was pretty happy in his furniture business, although now was a bad time for it. As far as he knew, he had done much better than Rae, who had moved in right away with a jerk named Eddie and sunk all her profits in him and his stupid charter boat.

So why is Nathan calling me now? Rae was thinking. She felt friendly toward Nathan but not completely friendly. For instance, if she'd really lost everything in the hurricane, she would've been sleeping under a tarp for months by the time Nathan called to check.

They had not parted on the best of terms, although their phone conversations always kept away from this. First of all, there had been the problem of Eddie, whom Nathan had never liked and had tried to urge her away from (had Nathan really thought she wasn't going to side with Eddie?). And then there was George, who was not a person but a gun.

What did Rae know about guns? Not that anyone had ever asked her. When they came back from South America, after that one time that they had been so jumpy and scared (and with good reason), Nathan told her, "Don't get so nervous all the time." All of a sudden he got silky and confident. If Rae left the headlights on all night, if Rae burned a cigarette hole in the couch, no problem. Let it go. Nathan as Mr. Mellow.

Tom, their old friend from New York, was staying with them in Florida, and one night after they'd driven out to meet some people at their favorite bar, Rae wanted to walk on the beach but she thought they shouldn't because they had too much cash on them at that particular moment. Nathan said, "No problem. We'll take George with us."

"Ah, George," Tom said. "Let George do it." Nathan opened the glove compartment, and there was the pet gun. A pistol, a revolver—Rae still doesn't know what it was. It looked huge to her—a blunt club, a live metal thing. What was she supposed to say? She didn't say anything. She let Nathan slip it inside his jacket and they walked out on the beach, which was beautiful at night, balmy and cool, with the lights of the city behind them.

After that Rae got shrill and cute and fake when she talked to Nathan; she sounded like someone who didn't believe a word she said. And she stayed over at Eddie's when she was supposed to see Nathan at home or to meet him and Tom at the bar. She didn't plan to be unreliable, but she got distracted.

Rae didn't blame Tom, whom she had always liked, a genial and sexy man. But he and Nathan were always speaking in low voices, always laughing in that soft, knowing way. "Whisper, whisper," Rae said, although they were not keeping secrets from her, only practicing a new style of discretion. Sometimes they called each other by different names. Nathan wanted to be Niall, of all things.

As Niall, he was certainly a better dresser. Things fit him better; he got hipper-looking eyeglasses. He had a leather coat that he was especially vain about. "Doctor Mr. Nifty," Tom said, whenever Nathan wore it.

In the end they punished Rae, for failing to arrive at the bar with something when she was expected at a certain time. It lost them a known amount, and they fined her from later profits; they were very fair and exact about it. They were fair people, or meant to be, and Rae said, "Okay, okay. Of course." She wasn't angry or surprised. But after that she wasn't a partner anymore.

She had known, of course, what not showing up meant. She had been out on the boat with Eddie, and he had wanted to stay out later and sail to one of the Keys. At night you could see the phosphorescence on the water, as the boat cut through the dark. It was her favorite time to be out at sea with him. Eddie didn't have to coax her—she wanted to stay out. She knew Nathan and Tom would not be happy. Still, for a good part of the night she forgot them.

And after that it wasn't the same. In their years together she and Nathan always said—on holidays, for instance—that they were family. Was this true? There were the Thanksgivings, great twelve-hour banquets with long tables of guests (better than getting stuck with anyone's real family). And there was the apartment, with all their stuff in it—the South American textiles and the cowboy cigarette lighters that Nathan collected and the mutual clutter of their clothes and newspapers. And there were all the nights of talk-talk-talk.

During the hurricane, when Rae was down in the laundry cellar of the motel, hearing the maniac wind break up the whole material world, she thought: how come I'm here all by my goddamned self? It was not a good time to be bitter, and she knew it. All right then. She thought about the men in her life, whom she dismissed and forgave and apologized to. One by one, she knew why they weren't there. But where was Nathan? Hey, Natemobile. After all that belief, all those seasons in different apartments, she didn't even have his phone number anymore; they had let go of each other as utterly as if they'd been lovers. All that pure voluntary love, washed out without a trace.

They had been through tremendous things together, although they had not always had the sense to know it at the time. Pretty hairy, Nathan would say. This is absurd, Rae would say. Do you believe this? Oh, boy, Nathan would say. Oh, man.

In fact, they had worn her out, those exciting troubles. She was weather-beaten when they were over. But down in the laundry cellar, with the pipes shaking, she was just as glad to be weather-beaten. All the disasters of her life (and Nathan was far from the worst) seemed reassuring, the grislier the better; she was glad to have them to remember. The trouble stored in her was like a white noise, another roar, to whatever was outside.

She was down there for a long time, next to the shuddering canisters of Tide and Clorox. She smoked cigarettes and talked to the cat. When the storm finally spent itself, she went out right away to the yard and the road. She was thrilled at the sight of other people and she went pretty wild yelling to the first ones she saw.

NATHAN'S FOUR-YEAR-OLD SON wanted him to get off the phone and do something. "Will you please?" Nathan said to him. It seemed to

Nathan he hadn't had a long conversation in years. He couldn't sit down, he couldn't do anything. He was busy all the time, like every other working stiff. Every minute had a task for him in it. "Get out of here, Zachary," he said.

Nathan remembered the years he spent with Rae as idle, with a few bursts of action now and then—like a long ambling conversation you could drop in and out of at will. They did everything at will then; that was the whole point.

His wife had said, when she wanted to get married, that it was too easy to let go of people if you didn't have fixed ties. There was a reason for binding attachments, she said, for vows and obligations. Nathan said he hated making anything legal, but he saw the truth of her position. You became each other's blood. His wife, his son. Blood thicker than water.

All the same, he missed, of course, those comings and goings of friends, the easy associations that were his other life and his other job; he missed Rae and Tom. Rae wanted to know how Tom was, did Nathan ever see him?

"He's fine," Nathan said. "Still with Laurette, and those twins she had from before—they're thirteen already. He's in Maine. They have a nice house they had built for them in Portland. Nice in August, in my opinion. Forget winter there. Even in summer you can't swim in that water."

TOM HAS A HOUSE? Rae thought. Apparently she was the only one still loose in the world. The orphan of the storm. It pissed her off.

"What's Tom's house like?" Rae said.

"Modern but woodsy. You know."

"I have half a house here," Rae said. "I rent the downstairs part. There's a yard."

"Too bad you didn't own something that got wrecked in the storm. You'd be collecting insurance money now."

"You bet. We could stake ourselves in a whole new business again," Rae said.

"Like looting," Nathan said. "We missed our chance."

Rae said what she was doing now was working for an agency that ran trips to Latin America. Puerto Rico, Mexico, Venezuela, Brazil. She was doing pretty well, actually, a lot better than she expected.

"Hey," Nathan said. "You got all your travel experience with us. I started you off. See that."

"Thank you, Uncle Nathan," Rae said.

"You were a good traveler," Nathan said. "You packed light, you didn't get sick."

But Rae was thinking about the hotel room in La Paz. The two of them had been stuck there waiting for some people who were many days late, which was a bad sign. A betrayal or a trap or a misunderstanding; in any case, she and Nathan weren't eager to leave the hotel. They stayed awake for days talking; Rae was not eating very much, and she felt bony and condensed; she could taste the tincture of her own bones at the back of her throat. Nathan's face looked long and somber and comical, like a dog's. They held hands, at one point. They tried to distract each other. After Nathan fell asleep, Rae tried not to listen to the street. There were the voices of men in noisy groups, and every so often the footfalls of someone alone, and then a kind of pulsating quiet. In the quiet Rae heard her own death. That is, she understood that her body was going to die, in a way that she never again fully understood since. She saw how her skin would be not live skin but just matter. Even now, remembering, she couldn't get her mind back to that point, that certainty.

True, she was crashing at the time, and just before she finally fell asleep, she was homesick. She wanted to be in her own room in Miami, she hated everything in the hotel, and she was afraid that Nathan was going to leave her there without him. Why did she think that? Nathan had always been trustworthy and there was no reason not to rely on him. But in the dark of the room she could tell how much she didn't know and what a raw, open pit of the unimagined lay all around her.

Now Rae could hear the noise of a kid in the background, at Nathan's house. "That's the baby?" she said.

"The baby's almost in kindergarten now," he said. "Go be a pain some place else, Zack."

Nathan was thinking how happy Rae sounded about her new job. He was always sorry that she hadn't stayed longer in the business, although she had avoided some of the troubles he and Tom faced later on. But Rae could've come out of it with more money, he always thought. She could've thought ahead better.

"Next time I'm spending thousands on travel, I'll book with you," Nathan said. "What's the most expensive thing?"

"Cruises are big," Rae said.

"So I'll book the *Loveboat*," Nathan said. "I'll wear a lei."

"Disney World," Rae said. "That's what you need."

Nathan's son was playing, very loud, a song sung by Kermit the Frog. Things sounded safe at Nathan's house.

To this day, Rae never expected to live in a house like that. Probably Nathan hadn't either, but he was more adaptable than she was. As it turned out. It had been too soon to tell that about anyone then; that was why so many people had seemed alike.

"With every *note* there's a lump in my *throat*," Kermit sang.

"I hate those goddamned Muppets," Nathan said.

At Nathan's house there was the sound of a woman's voice calling out something over the music. Nathan's wife wanted him to take Zachary to the park to tire him out. "They have a penned-in area for kids," Nathan said. "And then the rest of the park is for the dope dealers. Don't think it doesn't confuse me to be in there with the swings."

After Rae hung up the phone, she sat for a while on the wrecked sofa (which had been torn by a cat before the storm got to it) and thought about Nathan walking hand in hand with his hop-skip-jumping son. Doctor Mr. Dad.

But Nathan had always been ready for just about anything; nothing he might've done would have surprised Rae. He was a confident person, interested in many things. The night that Rae hadn't shown up at the bar, when she'd been out on the boat with Eddie, she'd wondered if Nathan might just forget that he'd asked her to meet him. Of course not, but perhaps he had an alternate plan, just in case she failed him; Nathan did think that way. On the deck Rae leaned against Eddie, whom she did not truly trust either, although she liked him fine. How circumspect they all were in those days, how flexible and wary.

It was a beautiful night, on Eddie's boat. The ocean noise was steady and pure in the dark, and she was really very glad to be with Eddie. Every so often she was uneasy, worried about Nathan and beset by the sense that she was being unfair to him, and unprofessional. What would he do, in her shoes? She had never thought of their arrangements as fragile; they had their code and their long loyalties. It was true that Nathan had once said, "Past a certain point, you watch out for yourself," but they were talking about what to do if one of them got arrested. And there she was, already watching out for herself, under the mere pressure of sexual love, as if that was strong enough to pull her away; as if either of them, all along, could float away on just that current.

Comforts

The video store where Rickie was manager did most of its business after five. She kept the place open until midnight on weekdays and until two on weekends. Saturday night was always what Rickie called monkey night, crowded and frantic and filled with long lines of jerks. "What hole did he crawl out of?" she would say. "Who got her socialized?"

"Every dickhead in the world is here tonight," Deanne would say. Deanne was Rickie's favorite of the clerks.

Rickie told Deanne to pay attention to how jerks were dealt with at the stores. How much more useful can knowledge get? People were allowed one or two normal questions ("Did you see this?" "Is this funny or not?"), and then if they kept on—a lot of people kept on, they couldn't stop—if they got into "Could you find me something like a western but that's not too upsetting?" or "Is Lee Van Cleef a Republican or is it just Clint Eastwood?"—Rickie would say, "This is not *Jeopardy*" or "Don't you have a home to go to?" Not clever, but effective. If a girl was busy prancing in front of a rock video, Rickie would say, "Madonna comes to our own neighborhood." The girl wouldn't stop just then, but she would fade out soon.

Sometimes there were arguments. More than there should've been in a video store. People got nasty back and Rickie got nastier. She was backed up by Vance, the Associate Manager, who got right into the spirit of the thing. "You can take that attitude out of here," Vance would say.

On certain nights, they turned the place into a bar without liquor, the two of them. Once someone said he was coming back with a gun to get Rickie, and the police had to be called. But this was on a very bad night. More often the late shifts were just ragged and long.

The staff spent a lot of time talking about what to show on the monitors. The younger clerks went in for heavy-action films. Blood, guts, screams, burning, maiming, shooting. They hooted and groaned in the worst parts. "That's so *cold*," Freddie J. would say, when some character blew away his uncle. Rickie could see their faces take on hardened expressions while they had lovely, relaxing daydreams of being that tough.

Rickie was glad on the nights Deanne was there to talk to. Deanne was a very sweet person, who went in for cosmetic distortions—white face powder, black lipstick, multi-pierced eyebrow. A style Rickie thought had peaked a while ago, but she noticed plenty of other examples walking around New York. Rickie liked to feel the shaved part of Deanne's haircut, which was like a dog's stomach. "It grows in so fast," Deanne said. "It's worse than having a lawn to mow."

Rickie thought of Deanne as dainty and aristocratic, despite the ripped T-shirts and the looped chains she wore hanging from her belt. Rickie kept offering her advice. "People like that waif look but you pay a price," she said. "Don't you?"

Vance was always hovering around while this was going on. He had his advice too. "Try brighter colors." "Loosen up."

"Don't be a nerd," Rickie said to him.

"Listen to me," Vance said.

Probably Vance's directions had a little sexual hope mixed in with them. Rickie saw how he made a lot of trips back to the storage room when Deanne was unpacking something. Deanne just called him Big Daddy. He and Rickie were both a good twenty years older than she was.

So they were all busy looking at the screens—watching a cop movie with a lot of mountain scenery in it—when one of the Saturday creeps came up to the counter. He was checking out *Lust's Chain Reaction* and *Blondage*. It was Rickie's theory that men like him shouldn't be permitted to rent those movies. He had dirty hair, cruddy skin, bad teeth; his connection to his own body was so off, in Rickie's opinion, that he shouldn't be encouraged to go rub it against anyone else's. He said to Deanne, "You want to watch this with me tonight?"

Deanne said no in a faint, sick-cat voice.

"This one has a dungeon scene that's famous," he said. "I was thinking about you when I picked it out."

A chill went through Rickie. Deanne started looking at something in the shelf under the counter. She rustled papers, she kept her head down.

"What do you say?" he said. "I can't hear you. I'm listening hard."

"Nothing," she said.

"I can't hear you," he said. "You like this kind of movie, right?"

"Excuse me," Rickie said. "You have to leave. Thank you very much, good night."

"I didn't think I had to leave so soon," he said. The clerks didn't think so either. They seemed a little startled at Rickie.

"You do," Vance said. "Believe us."

And the man did start to leave then, taking with him the videotape, which he had not paid for yet and which made the alarm go off at the door. The loud electronic ringing stunned the whole store and got Jean-Claude, the Haitian security guard, over there in a second. He made the man step back inside, and the alarm stopped.

"Get away from me," the man said. He looked breathless—his mouth was slightly open. Everyone in the store imagined how crazy he might get, and in the long pause the man himself seemed to be turning over the possibilities.

"Get out of here!" Rickie said.

The man threw the tape at the window, but it didn't do anything except make a clacking noise hitting the glass and falling to the floor. He said, "Bunch of jokers." And then he walked out.

Jean-Claude was ready to go after him, but Rickie said, "No! Forget it."

Rickie wanted the whole thing to have been a lesson to Deanne. That was her first thought. Look at Deanne—stiletto-heeled boots, gold rings up her nose, hair bleached raw. Tough enough for tattoos, but how come she couldn't do better than quake in that little pipsqueak voice? "Don't ever be nice to someone like that," Rickie said. She wanted to tell Deanne a few other things. Speak louder, stand up straight. Deanne looked blank and dreamy at the moment, angelic in a tense sort of way.

Deanne said, "I have to apologize for my friend. He starts out kidding but then he just gets like that. It doesn't matter what I say to him when he's like that, you know? He gets in a mood."

Rickie felt old and stupid. What I know about this you could put in a flea's ear, she thought. Handcuffs, blindfolds, getting tied to the bedpost; thousands do it, right? "So will he be back or what?" Rickie said.

"I'm so sorry," Deanne said.

Freddie J. came up and put his arm around Deanne. All of the clerks looked worried. They were a nice group.

"A little excitement to perk up our evening," Freddie said. "Why watch the monitors when there are guys like that around?" Deanne did some giggling at that.

But Rickie couldn't get a straight story out of her about whether the guy might be up for a revisit tonight. "He's a showoff," Deanne said. "It was so silly."

"Let him act out someplace else next time," Rickie said.

Vance said, "You wanted to tell him off but you weren't firm enough. That's the whole thing, consistency."

"Vance," Rickie said. "Thank you for your counsel."

No one in the store thought it was a good idea for Deanne to go home alone to her own house. "Oh, please," she said. "I've known him for months and he's fine. It was nothing."

But at the end of the night, when Rickie was ringing out the register, Deanne wanted to know how big Rickie's apartment was, how far away, and did she really not mind having someone stay.

Rickie had three rooms and she was set up okay for visitors, as long as they liked dogs. She had a couch in the living room, a futon, and a sleeping bag that could be dragged out if necessary. She had two grown sons, although they had never, in fact, both stayed with her at once.

The dogs went wild when Rickie unlocked the door. Johnson ran around in circles, Speedo lunged at Deanne, Brownie wagged her tail and peed, and Beverly wouldn't stop barking. "Doggies, doggies,"

Deanne said. Speedo started nipping Brownie and was sent into another room.

Rickie had not meant to have four dogs—who would? Two were from the street, one had been brought to her by a woman who heard she took in dogs from the street, and one was from the ASPCA adoption van.

At the moment the dogs were clamoring to go out. Rickie got them hooked up to their leashes, and when Deanne said she wanted to come along, Rickie made her take two of them. On the street Speedo was better; he stopped pulling and sat at the crosswalk with the others when she told him to. "Good *boy*," Rickie said, which made Beverly jump around and tangle the leashes.

"They have dark pasts," Rickie said. "Old traumas buried deep in their little brains."

"Don't we all?" Deanne said.

"We don't dig holes in the carpet and bite the fur off our tails when we're nervous, at least," Rickie said.

"I think they're doing quite well," Deanne said. "If they stayed still for a minute, you'd think they were normal."

Under the streetlights Deanne's dark lipstick looked particularly weird, and Rickie wondered if she would go in for that effect if she were twenty-two now. By the time she was Deanne's age she'd had two sons, and the oldest was almost seven already. And the second pregnancy had been on purpose. Where had she gotten that idea from? She'd had no shortage of ideas then, and not a single one of them had made anything easier for her. *Au contraire*, as Philip her son would say now.

Deanne said, "You feel safe walking these dogs alone at night?"

Rickie thought this was an amusing question, from somebody who hung out with guys who liked to talk sexy about dungeons. Two of the dogs were quite big, in fact.

"Why?" Rickie said. "You want to take them out at three a.m. for the thrill of it?"

"Oh, yeah, that's my kind of thing."

"You better be careful, whatever it is you do," Rickie said.

Rickie had to stoop to pick up some dogshit, so she missed the first part of what Deanne said next. What she heard was, "Actually, he makes me quite happy."

Yes, well, it might be elating to stumble on these unlit corners in yourself—Rickie could see that. Deanne must have thought she'd found a truth she could settle into. Her own rocky turf. It won't serve you well, Rickie wanted to tell her. You're underestimating; more will be required of you than you can dream of now.

Deanne, who must've seen Rickie's expression, said, "We always have safe sex, don't worry. Almost always."

Rickie gave a snorting laugh. Safe, my eye. Deanne looked insulted.

When they got back to the house, Rickie got out the clean sheets. She didn't say, if that guy is such a pearl, what are you doing camping out here? She didn't say a lot of things. When she opened out the folding couch, there was a clump of Philip's old underpants stuck in the crease of the mattress. Deanne made a hand puppet out of them, wagging her finger through the crotch. "They're my son's," Rickie said. "Please."

Rickie showed Deanne the good photograph of Philip, the one of him at Christmas. "My oldest," she said. He had a thin, severe face—he hadn't turned out as handsome as she'd thought. His half-brother Adam was the really gorgeous one these days—blond, sleepy-eyed, calm. As a toddler he'd been fat and funny-looking, with a shock of hair in his eyes like Dennis the Menace. My little fatty Addie, she'd called him. The infant tornado, always into something.

Deanne was putting the underpants on her head, an elastic-rimmed caplet with leg holes around her ears. "Is that your usual equipment?" Rickie said.

"Yes! I will drive men crazy with this," Deanne said.

But when Rickie came back to the living room with a bottle of brandy, Deanne was already lying in bed, under the covers, with her eyes closed. She must have had her clothes still on. "Good night then," Rickie said. The dogs sniffed at Deanne's arms and face. Brownie licked her hand. She couldn't be asleep already, Rickie thought; nobody falls asleep that fast. "You okay?" Rickie said. But Deanne lay silent, with her hand thrown across her face.

When Rickie woke up in the morning, Deanne was already gone. The first thing Rickie did was to check to see if anything had been stolen. Nothing had, of course, as far as she could tell. It was an old habit—counting to see what was missing—left over from the last year with her second husband. She would wake up in the morning and her radio would be gone, or other things—her panty hose, her belt, taken for handiness, not money. He was the last person you would expect to get into hard drugs. A decent man, mostly, but too easily embittered and too ready to comfort himself. When she'd left him, she'd felt brisk and clearheaded.

Deanne had left a note:

> Thanks for the hospitality. I know my friend would not have bothered me but it was very nice of you. The sofa is very comfortable! Thanxs again—
>
> D.

Deanne had a full day to get into trouble before work, if that was her inclination. She was, if nothing else, prompt about showing up for work, quite reliable that way. She said once that she'd been working since she was seventeen and the store was the first place she hadn't hated.

The dogs had gotten hold of Philip's underpants and shredded them all over the floor. Johnson had bits of white cotton all over him, as if he had rolled in the stuff, and there were thready clumps on the coffee table and on the leaves of a plant. It reminded Rickie of when the boys were little and she used to let them play tug-o'-war with old towels. In California, where she went when her second marriage broke up, the boys were sometimes stuck by themselves in the apartment when she went to work. That is, if the neighbor wouldn't babysit, Rickie left her son Philip in charge; he was almost nine, Addie was two and a half. The place was always a pileup of mysterious debris when she got back.

Rickie was working at the time in a health food store, a more lively place than it sounded. It was a big market, with a restaurant in one section, where people hung out and drank murky vegetable juices and dealt drugs and waited for things to happen. Half the town shopped there, the other half worked there, and Rickie had her own flirtations, more than she expected. She was then twenty-five, not pretty or unpretty, a solid-built person with a short mop haircut and a loud voice. (Too mouthy for California—she almost got fired the first day for telling a woman there was probably no avocado in the store good enough for her.) Rickie fell into what turned out to be a long romance with a man who drove one of the delivery trucks. They used to take the truck on her lunch break and go to the beach. They would lie around under a jutting rock, have sex with their clothes half on, and then eat their sandy sandwiches. Sometimes after work, too, they went back to the beach, which was especially beautiful in the later light. They could've gone home—he wasn't married or anything—but they liked it there.

But the boys would be wild by the time Rickie got home. Once she found the baby playing in the cat litterbox, which she knew was dangerous, although he was past the stage where he put everything in his mouth. But the sight of it was awful to her; she felt so sorry for him, left in this mess as his sandbox.

Her ex-mother-in-law, a nice woman, said she would take the baby for a while, if Rickie wanted. Rickie had hinted for this but hadn't asked, and when the offer was actually made, she felt her skin go hot from shame. Still she packed Adam up with his toys and his clothes and took him back on the plane to his grandmother's.

Within a year Rickie had lost the job, and when she had to go back on welfare anyway, she wanted to get Adam back, but everyone said no—the caseworker, her mother-in-law, and maybe Adam himself, who got used to new places well. He was still so little, and by the time he stopped being little, his idea of home was with his grandmother, and Rickie let him stay.

Of all the things she ever did, Rickie was always the sorriest for this. She was sorry at once; she would cry at odd moments, all of a sudden, at the store or at home. Philip was off with his friends a lot then. Perhaps he was afraid she would send him away too, but she would never have sent away Philip, her own boy. Not after the years they'd been through together. But if she could take care of Philip when she was sixteen, why did she have to let Adam go? When Rickie thought about this later, it was hard to remember why she had guessed so low about what she could do, why she had pretended to be someone giddier and coarser than she was. What kind of false hope was that?

From Adam's viewpoint, all of it was probably for the best. Of the two boys, he was the happier and calmer one now. He still lived in Rhode Island, near where he'd grown up. When he came into the city to see her, he looked so mild and young, a nice man in a tie who sold powerboats for a living.

The one good thing her son Philip would say about Adam was that the dogs liked him. And the dogs did. Whenever they heard Adam's step, they went even wilder than usual; at the doorway Adam would crouch down and let them jump all over him. They licked his face; they squealed and whined. "I probably just smell," he said. "I think that's it." Rickie would stand over him, as if she were the only steady one, the looming maternal shape, waiting. Philip once said she looked like a dazed cow at such moments, but Adam of course didn't speak to her that way.

At the store Deanne was very chatty and sweet the next few days. She did a lot of little favors for Rickie; she reshelved sections that were always out of order, she brought Rickie coffee and surprise snacks. She made new signs, with illustrations, explaining the check-out and return procedures for customers. (How We Do It, the Magic That Is HitsVideo.) There was a cartoon drawing of Rickie as the mad queen, Vance as a bearded elf.

Rickie thought maybe Deanne was in such a good mood because she had dumped the bad boyfriend, but Deanne said, "Certainly not."

In any case Deanne was more tied to the store now. She came to work wearing a T-shirt that said *Video Vegetable*. She let Freddie J. explain in detail how they did the special effects for some particularly grisly horror movie. And she and Vance made up different nicknames for customers. *Willard the Rat*, *Bart Simpson Grown Up*, *Kitten with a Whip*.

They were starting in one night on a long-faced young man in a black leather coat. Deanne had already said Future Flasher and Vance was about to say more, when Rickie said, "Guess what? That's my son." It was Philip, come from the class in carpentry he taught at the Y.

"Hi, Mom," he said.

"You don't look related," Vance said.

"He's my grandfather, really," Rickie said.

Philip ignored all this, as usual. "I got the gates," he said. Philip believed that Rickie's apartment was underprotected from burglars, and he wanted to install iron grillwork on the windows, strong but decorative.

"I don't need the gates," Rickie said. "I have four dogs."

"What about when the dogs are out?"

Rickie was going to ask how she had raised such a worrier, but she didn't actually want to hear the answer. He had already put in smoke detectors. Next there would be red signs for the exits, for the parent who can't find her way out of a paper bag.

"I hope the gates don't look too prisony," Rickie said.

Deanne said, "She has a nice apartment. Don't you think so?"

Rickie saw her son give Deanne a long glance. Today Deanne was in a leather vest and a black tulle skirt like a long tutu. He said, "*Architectural Digest* is coming to photograph the place next week."

"Philip built the table in the kitchen," Rickie said.

"It's a great table," Deanne said.

"I'm a whiz," he said.

"He's making a good living with that furniture," Rickie said.

"Anything else you want to tell them?" Philip said.

A customer came up to bother them and Deanne had to go find a tape for him. Vance said, "Nice haircut on her, huh?"

Philip wasn't startled by Deanne; it was hard to surprise Philip. "That ballet thing she's wearing is cute," he said.

This was not much to go on, but as soon as Philip left, Rickie got interested in the idea of Philip and Deanne as a couple. It was a satisfying notion. Deanne might expose him to a few bad habits, but there wasn't much Philip hadn't been around already, and he had spent most his life being impervious. He could help her out of that swamp she was in and she could wake him up a little.

Rickie was so caught up in thinking this through—figuring out how to hint and plot—that the next night, when she saw Deanne leaning over the counter to speak closely to a male customer, Rickie's impulse was to go over at once to interrupt this flirtation. When Rickie got closer, she saw, to her outrage, that it was Deanne's boyfriend she was talking to. He had cleaned himself up a lot; he looked almost normal, in a gaunt, rodentlike way. He and Deanne were discussing something that involved a lot of chuckling between them. Rickie tapped Deanne on the shoulder and said, "Excuse me. I need you in the back."

When Rickie got Deanne into the stockroom, she said, "Listen. He can't come into this store. That's it. Forget it."

"He's not doing anything," Deanne said. "He's not bothering anybody."

"He's not allowed in here."

"Of course he's allowed. But he's going in a minute anyway," Deanne said.

"I don't want to see him here again. I can't believe he is in here again."

But when they came out he was already gone. Deanne said, "See?" and Rickie looked at her in high annoyance. She really was quite disappointed in Deanne.

And the boyfriend turned up again a few nights later. He came back on Tuesday, and he was gone before Rickie had a chance to get to the front of the store. "He has a legal right to be here," Deanne said. "A store can't refuse service."

"Don't tell me what service can't be refused," Rickie said. "You should think about that one yourself. In your off-hours."

Deanne got pink in the face, although Rickie would not have called this a blush. "I don't do anything I don't want to do," Deanne said. "If you really want to know."

"Oh, come on," Rickie said.

"If you were wearing a bracelet," Deanne said, "and it left marks on your arm but you wore it anyway because you liked it, that would be okay because it was your choice. Right?"

"You are betting on the wrong things," Rickie said. "Anyone can see that. And you'll be sorry later on. That's all I have to say. I know it's a free country. Big deal."

Deanne said, "Why are you so nasty to me?"

Vance came up at that moment, and neither Rickie nor Deanne wanted him to hear. It embarrassed Rickie, in fact, to think that she was just another advice-giver, another Vance always needing to put his two cents in, full of easy confidence and high volume.

Actually, Rickie had always been like that, a bossy talker. She couldn't stand seeing someone else's wrong decisions unroll in front of her. *Hey!* she had to say. *Where's your brain, stupid?* Philip, if he were here, would say that she had no reason to think she was so right all the time.

THE BOYFRIEND DIDN'T TURN UP again the next night or the night after. And Deanne was sweet as pie. She kidded around with the other clerks; she made the store quite pleasant to be in. She set up an area in the stockroom with chairs, where a person could sit during her break if she didn't want to go out, and Vance referred to it as her salon or her nest. Even Freddie J. said he expected to come in and see a sampler on the wall, God Bless Our Home.

But on Friday night, around midnight, the boyfriend showed up again. The store was not crowded; it had a tired, party's-over feel to it, a sleepy dullness. The boyfriend greeted Deanne by patting her on the ass. "Absolutely not," Rickie said. "This is a public place."

"What?" Deanne said.

"You heard me," Rickie said. "And he has to leave anyway."

The boyfriend turned around then and gave Rickie a dead-eyed look.

"You," Rickie said. "That's right."

He kept rubbing Deanne's behind. "Do you want me to leave?" he said to her.

Vance said, "The manager is urging you to depart."

"Tell them I don't have to go," the boyfriend said to Deanne.

"He doesn't have to go," Deanne said. "Why should he have to go?"

"Out," Rickie said. "I mean it." She could get the guard, but then it would be a real fight. She looked over to the door, to where Jean-Claude sat reading a newspaper. Everyone saw her look.

Freddie J. said, "Let the man stay if he's quiet. Leave it alone."

"He's not staying," Vance said.

"If he goes, I have to go," Deanne said. "You know that."

"See if I care," Rickie said. "But don't come back. Is that clear?"

"I'm gone," Deanne said. "I'm already out of here. Got that?"

She went to the back to get her jacket. Her boyfriend seemed to think about following her but instead he stayed where he was. The monitor was playing a rock video behind him. He turned and looked at it as if he were waiting in an airport.

The sight of his back made Rickie want to push him. When

Deanne came out of the stockroom with her jacket, Rickie said, "Your life is a mess."

Deanne's mouth looked set and hard. "You should talk," she said.

Neither of them sounded like herself. They hardly moved their mouths; their voices were flat. They sounded smug and menacing. Who did they think they were?

Perhaps Rickie had always been this person. How much did she like anyone else in the world, how much was anyone worth anything? What she wanted was to keep saying things in this voice. She said, "You can't go soon enough for me."

Deanne looked like a cartoon of scowling bad temper. Rickie did too, probably, with her arms across her chest and her chin out. So what, so what, Rickie thought to herself, and for a moment this was the sweetest of all comforts.

"Hey, Dee," the boyfriend said. "Let's get out of here."

And Deanne walked out with him, striding faster than Rickie would have thought possible in boots with those heels.

When Philip stopped by the store a half-hour later, Rickie told him, "I made a mess."

Philip thought she meant the store, which looked the way it always looked after a long, hard Friday. "Don't worry," he said, to be nice. "Where's the vampire ballerina?"

Rickie gave him all the gory details—how Deanne had said this and she had said that. Philip was quite a patient listener. Freddie J. looked embarrassed and walked away.

"Oh, well," Philip said. "She'll be all right, won't she?"

"You think so?" Rickie said. "Why do you think so?"

"She's a spry young thing," Philip said. Philip was maybe five years older than Deanne, the wise old man of the mountain here. But Rickie thought it was good that he expected people to hold up, to stay in one piece in the face of adversity; this had to be a sign of something okay in his past.

For years she had been afraid of how Philip was going to turn out. And he had ended up solid, a staunch and tolerant soul; maybe, at worst, a little incurious. She had to be grateful for that.

Rickie thought of Deanne, that spry thing, set loose on the streets with that jerk boyfriend, whom Rickie had turned into the hero of the night. Deanne would be marching along, with her collar up, muttering against Rickie, looking pinched and sullen. And even now, when Rickie thought of her, when she could guess exactly how Deanne sounded, she couldn't imagine what else could possibly make Deanne feel better than this did. She could do what she wanted—she could go too far—it was her own fucking business. How refreshed she must feel, how alert and steady, to walk along knowing that.

The Dollar in Italy

Jill isn't sure why her ex-husband is coming to visit. It's fine with her, as long as he doesn't stay too long. Tiziana, the neighbor upstairs, has suggested that a father who visits should pay child support—why doesn't Jill ask Bob for money? Jill has told her this would be like squeezing blood from a turnip, a phrase that was tough to translate into Italian. Bob is okay, Jill says. Tiziana doesn't believe her.

A lot of people are traveling these days. They stopped when the Gulf War was on but they started up again when the dollar rose, and they're still at it. In Rome, where Jill lives, the airport is busy now. It looks like a shopping mall on a heavy Saturday, except that uniformed guys with machine guns are standing around the entrance. Jill has not brought Lisa, her daughter, because she still thinks the airport is one of the unsafe spots. Lisa, who is seven, is waiting with Tiziana and is probably driving her crazy.

A throng of people walk into the roped-off Arrivals area, and Bob is there with them. He has a big canvas duffel slung over his shoulder. Jill waves. He looks dazed and rumpled, the same way he always looks. When he sees Jill, he seems startled, not as happy as she expected.

What did she expect? When they reach each other, they hug and do a fast, friendly kiss. He is getting a little bonier around the nose and looser around the chin—older. Her too; so what. "Hey," he says. Jill asks how was his flight? How bad was it going through customs? Did he bring Lisa her Ninja Turtle watch? Jill is going to have to do all the work of talking until he decides to wake up more. Everybody else on his goddamned flight looks combed and eager and fresh.

Jill can never decide whether it's better to like him or to set herself against him. Her ex-beloved. What about the eight years she lived with him—are they a mistake and a stupid waste, a dead loss? And what does that mean? What's gone, what did she miss by being with him? And here she is now; so what.

He likes Rome. The last time he visited he talked about getting an apartment here, to be near Lisa. It was just talk, the kind of thing people say when they've eaten well and they're walking up a hilly street with the umbrella pines in silhouette. Jill can't believe he'd leave New York for long, and she hopes he hasn't mentioned any of this to Lisa.

Jill has a tiny rattletrap car, a rusted-out thing that her friends call one of the ruins of Rome. Last time Bob spent half his visit taking it apart and putting it back together again; he made it worse. "Hello, Baby," he says now to the car.

When they pull up outside Jill's apartment building, Lisa is looking out the window and shouting down at them in her little yelpy voice. An old woman on the street scolds Jill for letting her daughter lean out like that, and then she shouts up at Lisa. Lisa looks subdued. But when Jill and Bob go up the stairs inside, Lisa is running down to meet them. She shrieks at the sight of her father. She is all over Bob, a little whirlwind of daughterly ferocity, an imp of desperate love. Bob is in heaven, as happy, Jill thinks, as he will ever be. Jill can hardly watch.

"Hey, Lisa," Bob says. "Your hair is different. Let me think. Was it blonde before? You dyed it, right?"

"It's *longer*," Lisa says. "I have long hair."

"You sure it's always been brown?" Bob says. "Maybe it was red. I think, yes, red."

"It was *purple*!" Lisa decides. "Purple and green. You don't *remember*!"

They go on like this for a while. Jill gets coffee ready. Lisa has gotten to the Ninja watch and is eating a roll and talking at the same time. In her school there's a boy named Beppe and he's a *stupido*. (Lisa has a crush on him, which means she likes to hide and shout gross insults at him during playtime, usually words having to do with vomit.)

Lisa goes to an American school, but a lot of the kids are Italian. English will be an asset for them later, their parents think. In the schoolyard they all revert to Italian. Lisa has picked up some amazing slang, metaphors Jill can't decipher and it's just as well. During the Gulf War there was a bomb threat at the school, and a guard stationed outside. A lot of the Italian kids left the school. Beppe left but he came back.

Jill might have taken Lisa out of there too, but it so happens that Jill teaches there herself. She did what she could to be safe. She didn't bring Lisa to the American Express office, to McDonald's, to the English-language movie house. On the street she had Lisa speak to her in Italian.

Bob didn't know about any of this. It was during one of his silent periods. The war in the Gulf got fought and settled without any word from Bob. Lisa tried to phone him—she was old enough to do this—but he was never home. Even later he wouldn't say where he was. Out of town, with a girfriend, just busy, who knows? Jill doesn't want to know anymore. She doesn't want to bring this up again—what's the point?—but if he stays too long she will.

Lisa is showing him what she got for her birthday. It's a doll that looks just like a little hooker; that's what she wanted. Jill doesn't believe in imposing good taste on a seven-year-old. The doll is wearing a gold lamé dress and what used to be called go-go boots. "Guess how much it cost," Lisa said. "*Cinquanta mila lire.*"

Bob clutches his heart and pretends to fall to the floor in a dead faint. "*Cinquanta mila . . . madonna.*"

"You spent that much?" he says to Jill when he sits up. It was her money. What is it with all these Americans who think she's living in some backwater where everything is dirt cheap? How come they're so surprised all the time? At school one of the teachers said she walks around feeling like money is bleeding out of her veins. She said this in class and it frightened Lisa.

At the moment Lisa has Bob wedged against the wall and is clambering over him like a Lilliputian. Bob says he didn't sleep at all on the plane. He's been up for over thirty hours. Maybe he'll take a nap soon. "You can't," Jill says. "Sleep now and you'll have jet lag for a week." She makes him get up and walk around. She gets him to drink more coffee.

Lisa instructs her doll to keep Bob awake. The doll walks around on Bob's head; the doll bips him on the nose. The doll dances up and down on a fairly touchy part of his lap. "Don't go to *sleep*," the doll says. Lisa is drinking coffee too, a taste of it in a mug of hot milk.

Bob is out cold on the sofa by noon. He lies with his face down, his ponytail tucked down like a feather. Lisa is disappointed and has gone back upstairs to Tiziana's to sulk. Jill reads a magazine in the kitchen, as if she could forget he's sprawled out and breathing in the next room. It's ridiculous that he's here except that hotels are expensive (everything is expensive here now) and Lisa needs to see him. But Jill is afraid of what she'll say to him by the end of the week, either in anger or in that terrible fake eager agreement.

They're not a good combination. She is worried about what will happen if they stick around each other too much. They once set a building on fire together. By mistake; hardly anything they were doing then was on purpose. They were using a woodstove in their loft, and the stove was hooked up to a chimney that hadn't been cleaned in probably fifty years. It was a drafty loft with one weak radiator and the stove made it cozy and homey. They knew enough to always put out the fire before they went to bed except that night they were fighting and they didn't. They were fighting about who was a selfish, unbearable person. Lisa was a tiny baby then. They woke up when the dog started barking (Bob still has the dog, a big Lab named Krypton). Jill remembers a feeling like a razor in her heart once she knew what the smoke was; Bob was pouring water at the wall and shouting to her. She got Lisa in a big blanket and ran out with it held over both of them like a tent. The smoke wasn't so bad, but Lisa was making those little hollow baby coughs under that wool tent.

On the street the weather was cold enough so that when the fire trucks doused the building, the water froze on the brick in icicles. Everyone from the building hovered around her and Lisa; they kept asking about Lisa. Jill was trying to find Bob. When she saw him by a lamppost, with the dog running around at his feet, they looked across at each other—stricken, crazy, ruined. It did not help that they were in the same boat; it was a horrible boat.

They got Lisa to a hospital and she was all right. As it turned out, the building was all right too. The worst damage was in their loft and the neighbor's, both without smoke detectors. At the time, Jill remembers, she was so glad that no one was hurt; she thought she had never known before what being grateful was. Later the neighbor wanted to sue them, and the landlord made threats. She and Bob were living in Brooklyn then, the worst time in Jill's life, while the legal snarls went on between insurance companies. These may still be going on, for all Jill or Bob knows. Neither of them has held an apartment in their own name since then.

For a while, when Jill first came to Italy, she really did sort of forget about that time. She was with Giancarlo then, and while his English was good, their conversation had certain limits of vocabulary, of convenience. They stuck pretty much to the here and now. His friends lengthened and repronounced her first name, which does not sound like a name to Italians; forget Jill. But now it's the same as if she were anywhere; she walks around with her underlayers of old feeling, her sudden jolts of memory.

She's lived in Rome for four years now. Things have happened to her here—she has spots all over town where she was blissful or miserable with Giancarlo. Giancarlo always said he didn't like Rome. He used to complain that Rome was too unmodern, too crowded with other centuries. When he was a teenager he rode his *motorino* through the Forum for spite; he wrote graffiti on the walls of churches. He regrets that now but kids still do it. Maybe Lisa will be one of those teenage vandals, if they stay here that long.

Jill was a teenage runaway herself. At sixteen she was in New York working as an exotic dancer. She still has a tattoo from that time, a blue rose above her left breast. Bob loved it. Giancarlo was not too happy when people saw it at the beach. Only recently has it fully occurred to Jill how surprising it will look when she's an old woman—a blurred inky flower on her skin. If she takes a new lover at seventy, she'll have to explain it all over.

When Bob wakes up from his nap, he can't figure out where he is at first. He's lying on a sofa in a room with a terra-cotta floor. A rush of brilliant daylight is streaming through the window.

He thinks it's good he slept. At home he's used to being awake in the middle of the night, stuck in bed waiting for daybreak. In those hours he feels as if he's lying in a ditch. He hasn't slept right ever since the art gallery he runs started heading toward bankruptcy; this is not new for art galleries but he can't believe how much money he's lost. The sheer amounts, thousands and thousands, make him want to howl in agony. How did this happen?

He's had to do some things, like cash in his life insurance policy, which he promised Jill he'd never do. He might not tell her while he's here. He's never been good about giving her money for Lisa, and now he doesn't see how he can. Jill won't yell at him, but she'll be stony and disgusted. When they were getting divorced he used to think, no more fights at least after this. He didn't know beans about it.

Bob can't get over how much money he's lost. What if he never gets over it? At times he hears himself praying. He is not a believer and the prayers have no content. They're just names, a repeated addressal; it soothes him to speak on a plane that has nothing to do with money. But now he sees himself slipping into pleas and hope, attempts at private bargaining. Bribes are next, he knows. On Jill's block there is a little cement shrine built into the corner of a building, a dusty ceramic Virgin in a curved niche. People put flowers there, bouquets still wrapped in cellophane. These are requests. Bids for special favor.

And what if this sort of thing worked? What would that mean?

It frightens Bob to think of—so petty, so tricky. Bob wants to rise above things: isn't that what he's supposed to learn? He is here for the company of Lisa, which, like prayer, gets your attention elsewhere. (Although it's her money that's lost, if you want to see it that way; he doesn't.) With her hair long, she looks like an Afghan hound now.

How did her hair grow so fast? He is angry, when he thinks about it, that Jill keeps Lisa here in Rome. Why is Jill still here? She could move back now, without Giancarlo. He knows she isn't idling here to spite him, but she might as well be. Even on this crappy couch, he slept so well, with Lisa in the next room.

All week Bob takes Lisa to the park as soon as she gets out of school. It's a beautiful park, full of palms and cypresses and fountains and topiary. It has swings for Lisa, a slide.

Jill pictures Bob on a bench, watching Lisa as he's waiting for her to do him good. Lisa knows this or knows something. She's too lively around him; she gets really monkeyish and loud if he laughs. Jill would rather not see this. When she lived with Giancarlo, she used to take Lisa back to New York herself. She would stash Lisa with Bob and stay alone with a friend, be single and light.

At night Bob sleeps on her sofa now. The first night Jill brought in the blankets and the towels, just in case there was any question in his mind. But in the morning when she saw him asleep in his underwear she felt bad, as if she'd been mean and heartless. As if she'd made him go to waste. Someone should admire him, half-naked like that. Not her though. Let him cover himself up.

Lisa has been going through a phase of being curious about bodies. She spies on Bob at night, Jill knows. A few months ago she and Lisa were in a church with a dead saint's body miraculously preserved—beyond putrefaction, although it looked pretty black and mummified to Jill, under its satin dressing. Lisa, who has seen this sort of thing before, got very interested all of a sudden in the mystery of the flesh: Has anyone ever been born without skin? Are men's bones made of the same thing as ladies'? What happened to the saint's penis?

These are questions Lisa would ask anywhere, but Jill, being a mother, is sorry now that Lisa got such a long look at that leathery skeleton in its reliquary, the bitter remains.

Bob has made a few vows to himself. He doesn't want to become cheap, a worrier over spent nickels and wasted food, a high complainer and low tipper. If he gets like that, there won't be much left of him. Already he is getting a little like that, he can see. In restaurants he suffers great torments—he talks Lisa out of getting the prosciutto and melon and then he makes her eat an expensive dessert. He embarrasses Jill in her neighborhood trattoria by almost sending back liqueurs that are in fact free.

He and Jill are trying hard not to fight with each other. Lisa starts singing to herself when there are big silences at the table. She does "The Itsy-Bitsy Spider" in a small, mumbling voice. She tells long boring stories about Beppe and Jennifer and Luca and Miss Bridgewater at school.

She also has some brat moments, which distract them. She does *not* want her mother to order the black squid-ink risotto; she makes vile retching noises as Jill eats it. She does *not* want her father to tease her one more time about her hair, and she says, "*Stupido!*" to him with a small smile on her face. "Chill out," Jill says. "Right now." Bob suggests they leave her in the restaurant, a threat Jill never uses.

Lisa acts hurt—she comes over and settles down in Jill's lap, a tired baby once more. Jill doesn't remember too much about being this age herself. Later she fought with her mother, tooth and nail, and she believes that if she hadn't fought, she would have had no life except as a crushed daughter, a furious humiliated creature. But sometimes, when she's playing with Lisa, she remembers bursts of affection from her mother, things she had forgotten. Kitten-face: her mother used to call her that. How can that be?

Lisa is nuzzling in the crook of Jill's arm. Bob is busy adding up the check. Jill remembers when he was much more dashing and spendthrift—was that better? When Lisa was born and Jill's mother came to New York to visit for the first and last time, Bob took Jill's mother out to Lutèce for lunch. A restaurant like that must have terrified her, but how could he have known that? He thought everyone liked glamor; he was too caught up in that sort of thing, Jill thinks, but he was always gallant and free, an easier man.

Bob is thinking how he misses the time when Lisa was smaller, when you could make up anything and she believed you. A squirrel the size of a refrigerator—you couldn't get her to buy that now. She talks a lot now; she talks Italian to him for spite.

"Hey, spaghetti-head," Bob says to Lisa. "Hey, mop-hair girl of mine."

"He called me that before," Lisa says. "He *repeats* himself."

The waiter is hovering around them. For a moment Jill is afraid Lisa is going to call the waiter stupid or something much worse, but she never talks that way to strangers. Only to Jill and Bob and now the alluring Beppe.

"Moppo," Bob says, "if I didn't repeat myself, how would you remember all the interesting things I say?"

"Giancarlo *never* repeated himself," Lisa says.

There's a bad silence. Even the waiter looks worried about them.

"I don't think I know this child," Bob says. "Does she look familiar to you?"

Lisa wails in protest but she's still smiling her thin brat-smile. Bob is tired; it feels very late at night to him. What about Lisa in the next decade, is he up to it? Every day she gets older and stronger and better at stirring up trouble.

Jill really would like to leave her right here in the restaurant. Tiziana says Lisa is too young to eat out at night any way. But here they are.

On the weekend Jill goes to the park with Bob and Lisa. The weather is sunny and beautiful and the park is crowded; Italian kids are running around in their cute fussy outfits. The youngest ones hold balloons and look dazed. Infant boys are being coached by their fathers to run after soccer balls.

Bob is in a good mood. He has bought a copy of the *Herald Tribune* and is catching up on the day-old sports news. It makes Jill lonesome for Giancarlo, who used to try to explain soccer to her. When Bob groans over a score, she says, "I'm not asking." They lean back in the sun with their eyes closed, as if they were at the beach. Bob wants to know if she gets homesick, and she says not anymore, not usually. Also, Jill tells him, she likes teaching art to the high-schoolers, who chatter all the time but aren't hard to handle. Bob says, "Not hard for you," which is nice of him.

Lisa is running to the swings and wants to be pushed. Bob gets up and pushes in a good sweeping rhythm; he gets her soaring. Lisa swings for a long time, with her legs stretched out, and then she runs over the grass, through a brick arch which is part of the ruins of a villa. Bob thought it was fake at first, but they don't have fake ruins here. Jill hopes the sight of all these broken walls is consoling to him (if that's why he's here), signs of somebody else's rises and falls. His business must be in horrendous shape, from the hints he's been dropping. She should be sympathetic but she isn't. Jill is glad he has life insurance at least to take care of Lisa, since she doesn't. Otherwise she doesn't expect much from him.

Lisa is standing by the fountain. She wants to do one round on the kiddy car ride, and when she gets on it, she doesn't wave but stares ahead, with her hair blowing behind her like Snoopy's aviator scarf.

"There she goes," Bob says. "Our own hot-rod mama."

A woman watching her son gives them a sweet smile. They must look like a regular family, how could the woman guess differently? Jill doesn't think she and Bob should ever get back together but at times like this that fact hurts her feelings. Look at them, all rosy and fond. Look at Lisa zipping around the track, poor Lisa. And yet they could be worse off. They could be enemies; they could still be at each other's throats, she and Bob. Instead they have behaved as well as they could; they've tried to be decent in these later stages. So they have not, altogether, wasted each other.

The last time Bob was here, when Jill got sick with a bad flu, he brought her magazines, he drove Lisa to school, he tried to fix the car. She thinks of him peering under the open hood, tinkering blindly with the car's wiring—it's not a bad picture. She is thinking so happily of the back of his head, with its wispy ponytail, that she has to stop this sort of thinking, and she's glad when Lisa comes down from the kiddy car ride.

"Speed demonette. We're training you next year for the Indy 500," Bob says.

Lisa of course doesn't know what that is. When Bob explains, he says, "Just don't learn to drive from your mother."

"Excuse me," Jill says.

Bob says the car was fine when he left here last time. It's the way she rides the clutch that ruins it.

"I drive in Rome," Jill says. "That's enough without treating the clutch well at the same time."

Bob says he'll have to give her a lesson.

"It's my car," Jill says. "I don't tell you how to run your business."

"Thank you so much," Bob says.

Bob is here for three more days, she'd better be careful. But he started it, as Lisa would say.

Lisa decides Bob has to buy her an ice cream bar, and they go off together to the refreshment stand. Lisa comes back with chocolate smears all over herself.

"Bath time when we get back," Bob says. "I left the water heater on because I *knew*."

"Nobody keeps the water heater on all the time here," Jill says. "I told you before. You did the same thing last time." And Lisa's too old for midday baths anyway. He probably still thinks she takes a nap. "You leave the heater on all day while I'm in school," Jill says. "You leave it on all night."

"So what?" Bob says.

"And then when you finally go home I'll have to pay the fucking bill."

"Send me the bill," Bob says. "If it's so important."

"Maybe I will this time. I should."

"You're ridiculous," Bob says. "You are."

Are they going to start? Once they start going, they won't stop. They'll forget that Lisa can hear; they won't care. Lisa is right there, with a pinched, wincing look. "We have to go home," she says. "I have to have a bath."

They walk without speaking on the leafy paths, under the arcades of trees. The sun is pouring down on them, in vain.

"You're not walking fast enough," Lisa says.

"Know what we have for lunch?" Jill says. "We have that peanut butter your father brought us."

Bob says, "Did you ever get peanut butter stuck to the roof of your mouth?" He does the usual clogged diction—he goes into the whole routine. Lisa laughs; what a nice child. Actually, Bob is funny at this. Lisa is making a big production out of her hilarity. She is working herself into a choking fit of giggles.

They leave the park by the gate that leads right out into a busy street—cars are streaming by them from out of the tunnel that runs under the park. "This is so unsafe," Jill says. "I hate it."

Bob says, "It's not so bad if you know how to cross." How does he know?

Meanwhile Lisa is shouting at someone across the street. It's Beppe, she sees Beppe. He's with his mother, a pretty woman in a tiny stylish skirt. "Beppe!" Lisa shouts. "*Stai zitto!*" Beppe looks around amazed, as well he might, since he hasn't been saying anything and he's just been told to shut up.

"Beppe!" she shouts. "Your head looks like puke with ca-ca on it!"

Beppe stops at the edge of the road, listening.

"I see your pukey head, Beppe. Do you see me?"

Beppe yells something back at Lisa—something in Italian that Jill can't follow—and then it's too much for him; he lunges out. Beppe runs into the street right when a car is coming out of the underpass, and Jill hears herself and Lisa screaming. They can't see—cars on both sides are in their way—but there's a squeal of brakes.

When the road clears, Beppe is being hauled off by his mother, who has him by the elbow. He is still standing, which Jill takes to be a good sign. She waits with Lisa until they can run across the road—it is a very long moment—and then Beppe waves to greet them. He thumps

Lisa on the arm. He seems to be fine. The car is still stopped, and Jill sees that another car has driven into it and crumpled its back bumper.

"Oh, God," Bob says. The two drivers are getting out, about to yell at each other.

Jill is thinking how much worse it could be; they are all thinking that. Lisa is crying. Beppe's mother is kissing his head. Jill and Bob are looking at each other. Bob's face is wild and scared; Jill is bleary and worn-out. The two of them are remembering the night of the fire, what it was like outside their building. They remember how much they wanted to get away from each other, how different they believed their trouble was to each of them, and how they couldn't wait to have it to themselves. Now they stand at the side of the road and nod at one another; they speak to Lisa until she calms down; they know each other so much better now.

Covered

Victor looked slumped and paunchy, when I saw him again. I stood there stealing glances at him, which I had time to do, because he didn't recognize me.

I was shocked that he had gotten so old. My mother used to like to watch TV and point out who'd gotten fat or dried up, whose face-lift scars were showing. Why was she gloating? She wasn't young herself. But perhaps gloating is not all of what she felt in noticing these things. All flesh fades: for centuries, hymns were written with this as their main piece of news, and it was not considered depressing, but something instructional and even refreshing to contemplate. To my mother, the screen offered meditations on spilt milk, earthly folly, the long and winding road.

The sight of Victor was offering me some of this instruction for free. When I told him my name, he didn't remember me at first.

"Ruth," I said. "Lora's friend." He did remember Lora, whom he'd gone out with.

"She went to California," he told me, as if I didn't know. People think New Yorkers talk fast, but Victor had that slow, nasal kind of emphasis. "California," he said. "She had another kid. She's married."

This was very old news.

"California catches fire all the time and it's falling into the ocean from earthquakes. The state is a mistake," Victor said.

"I hope Lora's all right," I said. "You ever hear from her?"

He didn't. Why would he? "She's all right," he said.

THIS CONVERSATION TOOK PLACE in an art gallery, at a very crowded opening. I was standing around the drinks table, getting cups of yellowy white wine to bring back for my husband and me. Later on, Victor passed us in another room and stopped. "Did you know that Lora had another kid?" he said. "Really. She did."

"I know that," I said.

"She was an excellent mother," he said.

"She was." I had been having a perfectly interesting conversation before Victor drifted through.

"Do you know if it was a boy or a girl?" he said.

I'd forgotten. The kid was at least in high school by now.

"I hope it was a boy," he said. "She would've liked one of each, at least. She wanted a dozen. People don't have a dozen anymore."

Victor was not drunk, although he was clearly ready to go on like this for a while. He never drank anything but orange juice, in all the time I knew him as someone who showed up in bars every night.

My husband Tony and I went off to another opening. We got mashed against a wall, and we talked about how much money we could afford to spend on fixing up the loft. We loved these discussions, although our list kept growing longer and we hadn't done much yet but paint the walls and fix some holes in the floor. "Track lighting is still a good idea," Tony was saying.

And who should run into us but Victor again? "Ruth!" he said. "We have to stop meeting like this."

"How can we ever stop?" I said.

"Let's run off together," Victor said. "To California. Right now."

Tony steered me away, and we went off into a less busy corner, arm in arm. We had only been married for a month, although we had lived together for some time before. Still this stage was quite honeymoonish. Alone, the thought of him could send me into a state of dreamy adolescent desire; this steaminess made me happy and distracted. It was like a pure idea, an idea that he was an inexact form of; sometimes his actual appearance was jarring.

Tony liked the paintings at this opening better then I did, and he said he wanted to walk around and look at them more. I was standing around waiting for him to come back, not patiently, when Victor found me again.

"Is that guy the husband you had before?" Victor said.

I said no and that I had been still legally tied in with the first guy, on paper, for much longer than I should have been.

"That happens," Victor said.

"But now I'm a newlywed," I said. "A blushing bride, ha ha. Really."

"Congratulations," Victor said. "That's nice."

"It is," I said.

Victor said, "My wife left me."

What wife? I was going to hear. "Seduced and abandoned," he said. "That's me. The whole story." I thought he'd been following me around just to tell me this. He must've been at the stage where grief keeps spilling out; there's no talking about anything else. Everything else is just an excuse to get to the heart of the matter.

"My wife was from Virginia," he said. In fact her name was Virginia. Imagine people naming their kid New York or Flatbush—they wouldn't do it, right? His wife was much younger (Lora had been a lot younger too). In Virginia she was a farm girl, but she left the cows behind; she was a bright, capable person, not the kind who would hang around the dairy barn. But by the time she met Victor, she'd had enough excitement to last her. She was easy to live with, unlike some people. During the week she had an okay job doing graphics design. At night she liked to lie in bed and play canasta; they would play for cash or penalties. She made biscuits all the time, a food Victor learned to like. Although he could never eat them with that white gravy for breakfast, even if her gravy was very good, of its kind.

"She wanted a kid," Victor said. But she wasn't so young anymore; she was in her forties. She had to have a lot of tests. Victor was sort of hoping they would just tell her she was too old or too something. She took pills, she got shots. Then Victor had to have tests. It turned out he was the problem. They wanted him to have an operation. No knives, Victor said. Forget that. Right now. What about adopting? What about just staying a nice cozy twosome? Virginia said, did he think his body was some kind of exquisite perfect jewel that couldn't be nicked? Did he think the two of them boxed in alone together for the next thirty years wasn't enough to drive her insane from boredom? She said a lot of things, so did he. And then it began to seem to Victor too that there was nothing to their life together. Things dissolved. He couldn't remember how to conduct a conversation with his wife. He couldn't remember how they ever passed the time.

Of course, after she left, he remembered nothing but. Their

home seemed like some lively paradise of jolly tenderness. Where had it gone?

Victor stopped here as if he expected me to answer; he waited. Where indeed? I was remembering my own life, as if Victor had been a song on the radio. I was also thinking: How *did* this woman live with Victor all that time? What *do* people talk about? His wife had thought they needed tasks and higher duties, a kid to weigh down their lolling days of kisses and biscuits.

I wanted to tell Lora about it. Wherever she was. Guess what, about Victor? I could say. Wait till you hear. Not that Victor was on her mind now, I would think.

At the time we all met, Lora and I were waitresses. In the daytime I was trying to be a painter. Victor was one of the men who hung out in the bar. People killed a lot of time in that bar; they moved in for the night, week after week. Victor was a big storyteller. The men loved his stories; they would repeat his punchlines, mimicking the characters from his old neighborhood in hoarse voices, as if they had known these guys themselves. *Listen, kid*, they would say. Frank the Foot. Teresa Fat Mouth. After work I would sit at Victor's table; I was insane from boredom by the time he finished, but I was usually waiting around with a man who wanted to hear more. The waiting had its own interest.

Lora would be there at the table, not with anyone in particular. "I'm falling asleep in my chair," she'd say. "I could go home, right?" Lora was from Dayton, a place she claimed to have always hated, but she seemed midwestern to us, placid and sensible. She had a baby only a few months old, a little girl she had named Gabrielle Pearl. By Lora's own account, she had known early on that the baby's father wasn't going to stick around, and some people thought it was a kind of stubbornness in her to have insisted on having Gabby. But in her stubborn pregnancy, before we knew her, she had found a good cheap apartment, a floor-through overlooking Tompkins Square Park. A big family lived across the hall, and the oldest girl was willing to earn a few bucks babysitting overnight at Lora's. So Lora could stay late at the restaurant, if she wanted to.

One or two drinks were her limit, though. She wasn't a drinker, and she had to get up early; she wasn't out to see where the evening would lead. I would be nestled in the corner, preening and flirting, while Lora slipped away.

The next day I would wander over to Lora's house, to drink tea in her kitchen. We would all show up around three, the rest of us from work, the women. In the afternoons we were slow and unfocused, hung over and pale with sexual memory. The baby sat on our laps and tee-heed when we tickled her; she was a bright-eyed, fat-cheeked thing. Not for a second did we envy Lora. We were her friends, and her situation was pretty interesting to us, but we would not have been like her for anything. Not us.

Her kitchen, with its stripped-down brick, its sanded tenement floors, its repainted refrigerator, had been made snug and rustic by much work on Lora's part. I used to ask her, when was she going to get a barbecue pit, a dishwasher, a rotisserie? This was a joke. Lora laughed. My friend Donna said, "Fantasize about a Jacuzzi, at least."

"An ocean is what I want. I want a house on the beach," Lora said. "That's where I should end up, I think. I'm a beach person."

"Who's buying?" Donna said.

Lora had ideas for the house. A porch swing, an outdoor shower. She was quite definite in her plans. So we were all surprised when, on her night off, Lora turned up at the restaurant with Victor.

Victor? The wolf boy of Flatbush? I had never even seen her act awake during his stories. The two of them stood around by the bar; they had been to the movies together. Lora looked happy but embarrassed. She had to listen to Victor tell the plot of the whole movie to the regulars, but she added details. "You look great," I told her. She wore a halter top she had made out of bandannas. "She looks like a dream," Victor said. He sounded sarcastic.

But she liked him. She beamed when he was anywhere nearby, and in the next weeks she showed up for work cheery and bustling. We were full of speculations about their sex life. He was older than we were, a stocky man with a rigid back, not to mention a short, old-fashioned haircut. Not a free, loose kind of guy, but who could tell? Lora could, but she just laughed when we asked her. She said, "You people."

Donna suspected him of complicated, kinky practices, things that took a long time to orchestrate, dark games of a repressed spirit uncoiled. My guess was that he was fast, boyish, and quickly sated. In the mornings Lora made him breakfasts of French toast and strawberries—we did know that—and he ate them sitting up in her wicker-frame bed.

What did Lora do with the baby during these hours? I asked her about it. She went to the crib when Gabby cried; she brought her back to the bed. Victor did not hold the baby himself, but sometimes he patted her like a kitten. The baby stared at him; her eyes followed his mouth when he ate. He was her first man overnight.

What was Victor thinking, chowing down his breakfast with that gaze on him? Different things. He said, "Listen, kid, did you have breakfast yet?" He said, "What do you have to complain about?" He could not believe how fragile the baby's wriggling shape was, how she could not be left alone for a minute. Her naked body was like a raw, pulsing heart to him, like the telltale heart.

LORA WANTED HIM TO WATCH the baby for an hour while she shopped. "Not me," he said. "I don't think so. I'm sorry."

Lora said, "An hour. Less. What are you doing that's so important?"

"That's my business," he said.

Lora said she was disappointed that he felt that way about it, and they squabbled for a while, until she told him to leave. She had things to do, she didn't have all morning to waste on him. It was noon by then any way.

And that was that. No more Victor. He ceased to show an interest. No formal goodbyes were said, but the truth was evident by default. But he didn't disappear; he still came to the bar when he wanted to. He had friends to see; he had hours he was used to keeping there. People came there to find him.

More than once, when he turned up, Lora got tearful right in the middle of waiting on tables. She had to go to the back of the restaurant to calm down. I was embarrassed for her. I didn't like this way of behaving; it was what people had always thought women did. What purpose did it serve? In the ladies' room I told her to forget him. Forgetting did not seem that difficult to me. I had already forgotten a number of things, or moved away from them. I was springy, if nothing else. But for Lora, time was measured more precisely; now it was the fourth month, the fifth month, of her child's first year. I gave her a Kleenex but I didn't feel sorry for her.

Six months later, Lora left New York to go someplace in the West. Donna got the apartment. None of us wrote to Lora, but we heard, through the grapevine, that she was living with a man she had known before—not Gabrielle's father, somebody else. He was a sound engineer. They were getting married, they had a house in Laguna Beach. Any time we wanted to visit, Lora had room in her house. "She's set up," Donna said. "The woman is covered." (Donna thought Lora was crafty at heart.)

AND LOOK AT VICTOR NOW. Crying in his beer. Tallying his losses over and over, groaning and moping and reciting his tale, again and yet again. I was listening to him! He still had people listening!

His wife was never coming back, no matter what he did now. She was with another person, someone younger. Victor's eyes went blank when he said this; he started to forget I was there.

"Victor," I said. "Guess what?"

He looked startled and a little irritated. "Victor," I said. "Want to go have dinner? Want to have Thai food? We were talking about Thai."

Victor shook his head slowly. He didn't want to be consoled.

"Do you have kids?" he said. "You don't, right?"

I told him no, and he sighed, for my sake, in a way I found quite annoying. I was thinking I liked him better when he was a glib and callous oaf.

I was ready for Tony to come back so I could get the hell out of there and go home. When Tony turned up, I practically threw myself on him.

"You lovebirds," Victor said.

"That's us," Tony said.

"What's your secret?" Victor said.

"We have a hot sex life," I said.

This was a vast simplication, of course, and a goofy thing to say, an old-broad thing to say. Tony looked uncomfortable and amused. I'd blurted it out in a spirit of protest, a little snarl at family values. It woke Victor up at least.

"What else did she say before I got here?" Tony said.

"I'll never tell," Victor said.

"Really we're tame," I said. "Right now we're obsessed with interior decor."

Tony said, "Our loft is a very open space to work with. Ruth's husband once slashed up all the furniture with a knife, and most of it hasn't been replaced."

"Why did he do a thing like that?" Victor said.

"You don't want to know," I said. "He was mad about something."

"What was he so mad about?" Victor said.

"Nothing," I said. "Nothing important."

My first husband had moods. People thought we were one of those unsentimental happy couples, wise to each other, arch and knowing. The night of the fire, I didn't come home early enough from a dinner out with my friend Donna. I knew my husband wasn't going to like this much, but I'd tried to make a point of laughing him off when he was into one of his ridiculous rants. I thought I took him with a grain of salt. You have only so many ways of watching out for yourself. The whole time I was out with Donna, I forgot him but I didn't forget. By then I was afraid of him, but I didn't think well of this feeling. We were in a crowded restaurant with slow service. The hell with him, I thought. I ate some grilled tuna and listened to Donna tell about her job that she hated. She did a great imitation of herself not wanting to get out of bed in the morning. She flung her arms across her face; she burrowed into the tablecloth.

The later we stayed, the more I knew nothing good was waiting at home. Later my nonchalance seemed stupid—later people were full of advice about my attitude, and they were sort of right. And yet. I had all that practice in not worrying, and long service from it. It was what I had to rely on; nobody has that many ideas. And it was the crude form of a higher detachment, which it turned I was going to need for a lot of things. I thought about that now, looking out at the two men.

Victor wanted to hear more about the furniture.

"I saw the sofa he did a number on," Tony said. "Not a pretty sight, let me tell you."

And then it was my turn to get teary.

My eyes filled and I had to blot them with my knuckle; I was horrified at myself. Tony said, "Are you all right?"

"Fine," I said.

Weeping in front of Victor was the last thing I wanted to do, ever. I had the insane hope that he didn't notice, and maybe he didn't. He kept gazing in front of him in that dulled way.

Usually I was matter-of-fact about the last days of my first marriage (everyone has a sob story, and I didn't need to hear my own details over again), but sometimes I was randomly leaky. And never at a good time. If I could have, I would've worn pads under my eyes, like the wads Lora told us she put in her bra when she was weaning Gabby.

The rest of us didn't even wear bras, but Lora tried to make sure that she was covered on top; she had to wrap up. Careful as she was, Lora said that what she hated, *hated*, was walking down the street and knowing that if something slipped, your whole female front was drawn as two wet targets.

Ordinary

When Patty was younger, an uncle who could not understand what the hell she was doing with herself kept reminding her to get married soon. She was cute as a button but she wasn't going to live forever. (He didn't know then that Patty was gay, although he knows now and is fine about it.) "I have to say, what are you waiting for?" he said. "You like honesty, right?"

I do? Patty remembers thinking. Where had he gotten this idea? She didn't think of herself as an unusually honest person, and she wasn't that eager for other people's candor either. Given a choice, she'd rather let things slide.

She is probably franker now than she was then. As she gets older—Patty is forty-two—she gets more used to explaining herself and readier with terms at hand. All the same, Patty is perfectly comfortable with phony small talk and polite circumlocutions, with things left unsaid.

In the town where Patty lives now in upstate New York, people probably also think of her as a blunt and open sort of person. Anyone can see that she and Charlotte are a couple, no big secret there. Patty feels this so-called bluntness is a false impression, but it does cause people to tell her things. The guy at the gas station used to be a bad drunk and is in AA now; the woman who owns Ferdie's Lounge has a son who steals cars. Within five months Patty knows this.

Patty does like to be trustworthy, and the only person she tells is Charlotte. The two of them need things to talk about. They've never lived out of Manhattan before and aren't used to being alone together this much. When Wyona, their sixteen-month-old daughter, is around, they have plenty to occupy them jointly, but at night a certain stillness falls over the living room. The stillness is welcome when it first starts—Wyona wears them out and they've been working on the house and Patty has a new office job in Albany—so they like sitting around in a nicely companionable fatigue, hearing the summer night outside, the insects' thick texture of sound and in certain hours a very persistent, monotonous whippoorwill. Sometimes the raccoons fight, arguing in shrill blurts, like electronic noise. All this interests them both, but as the evening goes on, their attention starts rooting around for more material. It drifts back to the human realm.

"Kevin says they're having trouble at this church where they hold the AA meetings," Patty says. Kevin is the guy at the Sunoco station. "The church gets mad because people leave the place so messy."

"Don't they have a cleanup committee?" Charlotte says. Patty says maybe Kevin is on it, maybe that's the problem. The station is pretty funky.

"Kevin could send in a goddamn maid every night for the amount of money they charge people at that station," Charlotte says.

"Believe it."

"When did he drink? Was he living here then?"

"I think it was when he was married. The wife still lives around here. She has a house down the road from Fred." Fred is the other mechanic. Patty and Charlotte's car, an old Toyota, has had so many troubles already that Patty has spent hours at the station. Charlotte says Sunoco is going to give Patty a shirt with her name embroidered on it, she is there so much.

"Kevin told me the meetings get a lot of people. I think that's his social life." For a moment she and Charlotte both enjoy a secret smugness about being better off than Kevin; they have each other and their cozy house and are drinking cold beers right now. All the same they wouldn't mind being out with the crowd at these meetings. Also Patty has lied to Charlotte about how much the new valve job cost; she has underquoted the amount by a good deal. She thinks she did this to avoid hearing Charlotte rail against Kevin.

Kevin goes in for long chats—he is always taking a break and drinking a Coke and asking Patty if she likes it around here. Does she swim in the lake? Does she like the food at Mario's? You could not call this flirting, but it makes them both lively. They tee-hee about who in hell would order pineapple on his pizza. Probably this gets added into the hourly labor charge. Patty was with men when she was much younger, and at certain moments she has entertained the thought that if she and Charlotte ever split up, she would go back to being with men. She still has a bit of an appetite for them. On the other hand, it's okay with her if this appetite remains forever unfed. She is old enough to know that not everything has to happen.

Kevin likes to hold forth about people who abuse their cars. Patty is trying not to be one of them. They think everything is fixable, and then they're sorry—they get what they deserve. "Anything but that," Patty says. People do not think. His own kids act like they can trash everything they own. "That's youth for you," Patty says.

Charlotte has been stuck at home a lot because of their troubles with the car. She has taught the dog not to run in the road and has gotten very busy with the garden. Rarely has Patty seen an individual more in love with her own produce. Charlotte went in right away for exotics—opal basil, sorrel, white eggplant. Bugs got to some things, and there was a terrible morning in May when Charlotte woke to find the deer had gotten through the fence and eaten all the young shoots. Patty has mostly found the garden a big bore and was secretly glad to see it razed. But out loud she spoke bitterly against the deer and helped Charlotte fix the fence; otherwise they couldn't live together, simple as that.

Charlotte has looked—not too hard—for a job around here. She was a chef in New York, but she quit when they adopted Wyona, and neither of them is in a hurry for her to go back to work. If Charlotte gets work, even if she just does dinners somewhere, Wyona will have to spend some time in day care. Probably they would send her to the Big Bird Infant Playschool, which is held in the same church where Kevin's AA program meets. "Maybe she'll love it, who knows?" Patty says. At night they debate whether Wyona gives a hoot about other kids yet and whether a Presbyterian church is the kind of spot she could cut loose in.

"If one more thing goes wrong with the car," Charlotte says, "we're in a major bind financially."

"Let's just sit here and worry about it," Patty says.

"I thought we were richer," Charlotte says. "Why did I think that?"

They do often think they're richer than they are. Why is that? Patty asks. They eat quite stylishly, for one thing, and they used to travel, before Wyona, so they've always had a certain amount of savoring and idling, in their low-budget lives. Nothing wrong with this, Patty thinks—and here they are now, after all, with the sun in the morning and the moon at night—only they have Wyona to watch out for and they don't know zip about what anything costs in the country.

ON THE WAY TO WORK the next day, on the highway in her rattling Toyota, Patty feels optimistic again. There is an excellent rock station that comes in well for most of the ride, and it reminds her of aspects of herself that have not been entirely ruined by being here. She misses New York, but upstate is not altogether out of the loop.

Patty hasn't changed her style of dress—why should she?—and she walks into work in snakeskin-Lycra pedal pushers and jewelry made from bike chains. The office applauds. She is having quite a nice time at work, actually. Rudy the mail guy asks her if she's going to belt the boss with those chains. Patty says, "He'll love it."

The style of kidding is different here—yesterday Karen from the supervisor's office brought Patty a sandwich with a fake worm in it—but everyone's glad to have a new person who's lively. They make a lot of jokes about the state they work for. The state of chaos, the state of Nude Dork. The state's feelings are not hurt by these or any other remarks. Patty, at her computer, gets paid to watch how the state allocates funds for substance-abuse services; she is still startled by the amounts involved. Some days it irritates her just to see the figures; she's like someone on a diet looking at pictures of food. She would like to shake the monitor down like a piggy bank.

All around her people complain about how broke and strapped they are, either that or about what item they just bought. This is irritating in its own way, but it makes Patty feel like one of the most normal people in the world. Everyone in the United States is in at least as much debt as she and Charlotte are; the two of them are ordinary and average, it turns out. For the time being Patty is glad to hear this.

THE MAIL ON SATURDAY IS TERRIBLE. Patty and Charlotte get a big bill from one of their credit card companies and a notice about their property taxes. When they decided to move from the city, people warned them about all the wrong things. People thought the living would be cheap as dirt. They worried instead about Wyona, who is, as the form in the lawyer's office said, a mixed-race baby. In Patty's experience, there are very few people who want to be openly mean to an infant. The supermarket clerk calls her my little sweetheart; the man at the drugstore makes silly faces for her. And Wyona is a perky, sociable creature, as a rule. Only the teenagers ogle; they hang out at night in front of the 7-Eleven waiting for things to ogle at. The town is at the edge of the Catskills, not *that* far from Woodstock, and Patty thinks they must have all seen far weirder sights many times. Not to mention the MTV they get over their satellite dishes. Soon the Wyona family will be old hat to them, more evidence that nothing happens in this burg.

Among the adults in the town the most hostile thing anyone ever says is, "Who's the mother?" Legally Charlotte is, as a matter of fact, which is what Patty or Charlotte says for an answer. Conversation can stall at this point. If Charlotte is there, she will start nattering on about how many months old Wyona is and what words she understands. Charlotte puts people at ease by boring them into the ground, Patty thinks.

Right now Charlotte is pointing out to Patty that the mail today also has some fabulous items in it—a circular for the hardware store, a coupon for the Casa Paco Restaurant—but Patty doesn't think this is funny. Wyona is in a crabby mood too. She is sprawled on a blanket, throwing her toys at Patty and Charlotte; she has refused to take her nap. Charlotte wants to work in the garden, and Patty says she will take the baby for a ride in the car. The motion of the ride often sends Wyona into sleep. Patty needs to get some gas anyway.

Kevin is at the gas station (Saturday is one of his days, not that she's memorized his schedule), and he yells, "It's the mighty blue deathtrap," when he sees Patty in her Toyota. Wyona hasn't been lulled out yet and is whining from her car seat in the back.

"How's it going?" Patty says, but she is drowned out by Wyona, who is protesting this stop by squawking. "Hey, Crab Apple," Patty says. "It's okay, it's okay." Wyona is shrieking—Patty can hardly tell Kevin to fill the tank—and Wyona begins thrashing around wildly. Patty leans around to check if there's anything jabbing the baby—there isn't—and she strokes her and says cooing things but she keeps Wyona strapped in. Otherwise there'll be no getting her back in that seat.

"Bet you never thought it would be like this," Kevin says.

"No way."

"What did you think it would be like?"

"Quieter."

"People don't know. They have no idea." Patty thinks Kevin is going to talk about his own kids, but he says, "Everybody thinks it's so easy. It's a big fashion to go be a parent now, right? Anybody can sign up. People think they can buy human equipment for their lives and play house. They think they can be fake about who they are."

Patty is grateful now that Wyona is squalling at the top of her lungs. She is so stunned that Kevin has insulted her this deeply, this meanly, that she keeps thinking there's something else he might have meant by what he just said. She doesn't say a word when he gives her her change, and she drives off with the wailing Wyona.

SHE DRIVES WITHOUT THINKING, following the road, full of hatred for every ugly sign she passes, every stupid-looking house with old appliances in the yard. Every Ferdie's Lounge and Grill, every Adams' Guns and Ammo. Why did she and Charlotte ever want to come here; what were they thinking? Wyona, however, has stopped crying, and when Patty glances back, she sees that Wyona is staring out the window at the lake; her face is full of sweet intentness. The lake is bright and blazing at this time of day. Some men and boys are fishing in one spot, and farther on is a place where Patty can park the car. She is a strong swimmer and has swum across the lake, but not in this part. She takes Wyona out of the car, takes off the baby's shoes and then her own, and she wades in, swinging Wyona across the water and dipping her feet. Wyona gives Patty a suspicious look for the first second, and then she splashes and crows, protesting only when Patty stops. This is just the sort of thing Wyona goes for in a big way.

Patty makes several resolves while this is going on. She will never, never go to that gas station again. She will never again be so vain as to mistake the conversational drift of a venomous jerk. She will not blame a whole region because of one semi-recovering alcoholic lout, and she will think about this as little as she can.

In New York she would have handled it much better. She wouldn't have been caught so off guard. She has lost some of her powers in coming to a new place. *Who the fuck do you think you are?* she would've said. Everybody on the street would've gotten into it. *Just a fucking minute.* The whole ride back to the house, Patty knows in detail what she would have said.

WHEN PATTY PULLS THE CAR INTO THE DRIVEWAY, Wyona is asleep and has to be gently unbuckled and lifted out of her straps. "A narcotized baby," Charlotte says. "My favorite thing."

"I'm sick of the ridiculous prices at Sunoco," Patty somehow has to say. "It's depressing. There are other places we can go."

Charlotte is not dumb; she has noticed Patty's smiliness around Kevin. "They'll rip anybody off, those guys," Charlotte says. "In my opinion."

Patty can't bear to let Charlotte know what freaks and fakes Kevin thinks they are and how Patty had nothing to say to that, as if she agreed with him. Keeping this to herself, however, makes her sour and stilted for the rest of the afternoon. She and Charlotte work together on fixing the back steps, but whatever conversation they have is brief and utilitarian. Patty is as sore at Charlotte as if Charlotte had ordered her to shut up.

Their carpentry project is not fun—Patty hits her finger with the hammer more than once—is this their weekend? All the same, by trial and error, the job gets done. The steps end up looking more or less like real stairs. Charlotte wants to celebrate by making the two of them a knockout Italian dinner—she will use three kinds of basil, she will grill chicken on skewers of rosemary.

"It's good to fix things like the steps," Patty says. "For when we have to sell the house."

"You planning to put it on the market next week?" Charlotte says.

Patty says she has serious doubts about letting Wyona grow up around here. "Who will she be friends with?" Patty says.

Patty could have said a number of things to Kevin she didn't say. What about when his wife was pregnant, and he was in the backyard, drinking and listening to the radio, when she wanted him to drive her to the hospital, and he wasn't ready and he wasn't going until he was ready? He called a friend to join him; they drove to Buffalo to visit another friend, and he didn't see his first son till he was a week old. It's a terrible story. Kevin is probably sorry that he told it to her. He probably hates her for having heard it.

Actually, Patty has heard a zillion versions of this same story, in her old job at a drug treatment center and in life in general. In fact, she's sick of hearing ex-hell-raisers' personal sagas of how they screwed up their lives as thoroughly as they could; that's one reason she wanted to come to the country in the first place. It's old news to her. Who cares? What she cares about is Wyona having to deal with all the Kevins of the neighborhood.

Charlotte doesn't want to think yet about taking Wyona away from here. Patty says, "We're not fooling anyone. It's not for us, this place."

"Why not?" Charlotte says. "You think the old two-parent never-divorced family exists anywhere? Look at what they're showing on TV sitcoms now. The new normal is makeshift arrangements."

Really, Charlotte has done much better here than she has, Patty thinks. She is peaceful and confident, quite at home on their small patch of acreage, while Patty has lost a lot of her nerve.

ON SUNDAY CHARLOTTE GETS A CALL that the Chez Gorgeous restaurant wants her to come work dinners every Friday through Sunday. Patty and Charlotte spend hours on the phone with the church day-care people, who at first balk at taking the baby only on Fridays, and then by the time they relent, Charlotte thinks she doesn't like them. Charlotte goes to check out the day-care program, where Wyona throws pieces of a wooden puzzle around and the teacher leads the Hokey Pokey to Little Richard and Charlotte decides it's fine. Charlotte goes back and forth to the restaurant and is horrified at their oven. She is in a food dither; she talks about *bains-marie*, moisture content in butter, meat spoilage. Patty says it's like living in a refrigerator to talk to her.

Also there's a car conflict. Two people with different work hours can't survive on one car—how did they think they could do this? In the end they get Bill, their one friend who lives around here, to drive the baby to the church and then drop Charlotte at work. Patty will pick up Wyona and Charlotte later, at different times.

They are exhausted from working this out. "What are we, yuppies?" Patty says. Didn't they come here for simplicity?

Patty has a little conference with herself about simplicity. She will never have it, in her schedule or her character. She will always be crooked, curlicued, and evasive. Why does she long for it then? For she does want everything simple, plain, clear as water.

So on Friday after work Patty has to go pick up Wyona at the church. They have already taken to calling it St. Big Bird. Stimulation is what they think the play group will provide for Wyona, although Wyona was already plenty stimulated that morning. She threw her cereal at the wall and her applesauce at Patty's shirt, which Patty had to change before work. "I hope it *is* very churchy there," Patty said. "I hope they make her wear white gloves and a hat with a veil."

But when Patty walks into the church basement, the walls are covered with dinosaur pictures. Fast music is playing on a boom box—someone has decided that hip-hop is the right music for one- to three-year-olds—and Patty is the oldest adult in the room by about two decades. She is also among the latest; the place is about to close. Wyona is sleeping, but she's like that. She is in a crib in a row that looks like an infant chicken coop. Patty can see the red of her barrettes from across the room, and her tiny nose up like a periscope.

A woman with a hairdo like Loni Anderson says, "That's a bold one there. She did very, very well, after the first part." Wyona is still asleep when Patty carries her out to the car. The Bold Thing; she does look like an overspent reveler, lolling in her car seat. Only, the car won't start. Patty tries letting it rest. When she turns the key in the ignition again, it makes the same grumbling sound. She tries over and over. Sometimes the sputtering is louder and she gets excited, but then there's a sad fade-out, a fizzle of surrender.

"Oh, no," she says. "Oh, no." If the car dies, they're washed up. If the car can't be fixed, it just means they never should have done any of this. They've taken on something they can't do. The two of them aren't equal to this. They think they can be fake about who they are.

A car has just pulled up next to her, and when she looks over she sees that it's a red Subaru, with Kevin in it. Early for his meeting; he's very gung-ho. "Not this heap again," Kevin says.

"I thought you fixed it." Look how he just opens the door and makes her slide over in the seat, without asking. "What did I pay for if you didn't fix it?"

"I did," Kevin said. "It's just thinking of new ways to bring us together."

Patty gets flushed when she hears this. The air is charged and staticky; they are sealed in the car together. He is sitting next to her, fooling with the key in the ignition. "I paid for nothing," Patty says.

The car is doing what it did, coughing and gagging.

"Why don't you junk this thing and get a new car?" Kevin says. "Get something that's not a joke."

"With what?" Patty says.

"With money," Kevin says. "Write a check."

Kevin often talks like this. He believes that she and Charlotte are rich renegades from the Upper East Side, despite every piece of evidence to the contrary.

"Don't be funny," Patty says.

"What, did you spend all of it already?" Kevin says. "On what?"

First off, on Wyona; that's why they don't have reserves. The one thing Patty and Charlotte never joke about is the money they paid so they could have Wyona, the fees from the lawyer and the bills from her birth mother, Darice. It would be an affront to Wyona to complain about this, as if they were tabulating whether she was priced right. As if they were Fagins with an Oliver Twist, instead of Wyona's family. (All the same Patty is sometimes staggered by the way hard cash was involved, by the way a kind of bribe was offered and taken. If she'd had money herself, Darice would have kept Wyona, although she was eighteen and already had one kid living with her mother. Charlotte has said she tries to think of the money as a dowry paid for Wyona.)

Kevin gets out now and opens the hood. He has Patty try to start the car again and again. Other people have arrived and are standing around listening to the motor gag. One of the men says, "That's a sick puppy there."

"Stop!" Kevin says to Patty. "I *said* stop. I could lose my hand here."

"You think I care?" Patty hears herself say.

Kevin looks up at her, stunned, and for a moment they both look glassy and surprised.

Wyona is awake and whimpering from the back. Patty gets out of the car and leans in to lift her out of the car seat. "What are you doing?" Kevin says.

"I'm her fake parent," Patty says. "I might give her some unreal juice in a minute. But it's none of your fucking business."

"Great," Kevin says. "Nice manners."

The people watching them must think she's strung out and vile-tempered. Kevin goes out to his truck, and Patty's afraid he's leaving. When he comes back with a pair of pliers and a clump of wire, he's still talking. "People get so carried away with themselves," he says, under the hood. "They make their big moves, they act out their plans.

Then they have to face the truth. The truth will out. That's the hard part. Where will they run to then?"

This is not a sermon Patty wants to hear. She assumes it is meant for her, and the assemblage of people watching seems to think so too; they are gazing in her direction.

"Kevin," a man nearby says, "are you fixing the car or what?"

Patty feels as if the meeting has already started. They all know Kevin, and now they know her too, don't they? What she would like, more than anything, is to be able to just hail a taxi to take herself and Wyona out of here. She knows this is a childish wish.

"He's airing his views," another man says. "None of his opinions stay home gathering dust. Not for long." Somebody snickers.

Patty just wants more than anything for the day to go back to when the car still worked, and she has the horrible feeling that she is begging Kevin. *Just this once, for me.* All that is visible of him is his rear end and his legs, sticking out from the car, his skinniness in jeans.

Just then Kevin does something with the pliers and says, "Try it now." Patty is still bouncing the baby up and down. "Are you paying attention?" Kevin says.

One of the women standing around says to Kevin, "Want me to try?" She gets in and turns the key, and the motor grumbles and then catches. The car is running.

"Oh, my God," Patty says. "You fixed it."

"It'll be okay now," Kevin says.

"Believe that and you'll believe anything," Patty says. But she gives Kevin a clear smile. She's pretty happy, now that her car starts. Maybe they can progress to a hostile kidding relationship. This is not the last time they'll see each other.

"It was in the electrical system." Kevin is not smiling.

"What do I owe you?" Patty says.

Kevin thinks about it. "Fifty dollars," he says. Someone standing nearby laughs. This is when Patty knows that she and Kevin will never be friends.

BUT WHAT DOES THIS MEAN for Wyona? That's the question Patty and Charlotte keep coming back to, on the way home from Charlotte's new job. Patty has told her the whole story, spilled the entire beans, while they were driving along in the car (which does seem to work fine) on a winding road in the cricket-filled dark. Charlotte is insulted that Patty didn't tell her any of it before. She's also annoyed to have to deal with it now after a long hard night in a strange kitchen. Charlotte smells of sweat and meat smoke.

Patty says she feels much better after speaking rudely to Kevin. "It did me a world of good," she says, "audience and everything," but this isn't all of it.

"He won't forget that you did it with an audience," Charlotte says.

"How is Wyona going to live here?" Patty says, not for the first time. "With the other kids. What have we done?"

In truth, they don't know what they've done. They can't tell yet. Any kids Wyona's age aren't saying much yet. Patty steals a quick glance at Wyona, who is in her same old car seat, sort of asleep. She looks fat and oblivious, with her head slumped into folds of chin; she looks like a cosseted Eastern potentate.

Patty thinks how sentimental they have been, inspired by the sweetness of everything surrounding babies. Did they dream they were moving into a Mother Goose landscape, a lullaby of fresh air and green pastures?

For a second she blames Charlotte, who is the sappier of the two of them, the more home-loving and the more hopeful. "You are so naive," she says to Charlotte.

"Don't start," Charlotte says. "I'm just in the mood."

They have been more careful than usual about not fighting here, as if they were on a trip and didn't want to spoil their vacation, and now Patty feels that thrill of not knowing what either of them will say.

"Why did you think we could do this? What kind of fantasy trip were you on?" Patty says.

But Charlotte says, "I'm so tired."

Charlotte's voice is scratchy, and Patty can gauge the physical weight of her fatigue; they do know each other. In the dark boxy unit of the car, the forms of all three of them seem suddenly very real to Patty. She is shocked by their live solidity, as if the audacity of their family group were fresh news to her.

Patty remembers almost nothing from the months when she and Charlotte talked day and night and decided all this. They had no idea. How could they have? Who could? Patty is not sorry, not a bit, but she feels that she was half-asleep through all of it and she is blazingly alert now. She has that jagged restlessness she used to get the night before exams, except the exams are going to last for the next twenty years.

From the backseat she can hear Wyona sighing in her nap, like a little old man. Bold Thing Wyona, their own girl; Patty feels smitten and frazzled, a fool for love after all. She turns onto the gravel side road where their house is; at night this spot is always like entering a dark tunnel. Patty thinks back, with sudden nostalgia, to the time when she never had to drive, before she moved up here, but already she can't quite remember it.

First Marriage

When I was growing up, I had a Great-Aunt Faye who had been in a bad mood for decades. Her one expression was outraged disgust; she would groan about her clogged sinuses and her Peeping Tom neighbors and the messy habits of her husband, Abe, who was remarkably nice to her. He would take Faye, with her thin, dyed, auburn hair and hard-penciled eyebrows, and gently lead her by the arm through all the family parties, where she couldn't eat whatever the food was and couldn't stand the noise of children. Uncle Abe kept hard candy in his pockets to give to us. When we whined, our mothers always told us we sounded like Faye.

When I was in junior high, Uncle Abe walked out on Faye; he moved out of their house. None of us could believe it. Now, after all these years? They were so old by then, we thought, although they were probably still in their fifties. Go, Abe, I was thinking. Do it now. Nobody felt sorry for Faye; she was a hard person to feel sorry for.

Abe did have someone else on the side, it turned out, a woman from his office. And Faye improved, after this, or she got quieter, which for us was the same thing.

I used to like this story, which proved that a miserable person can save his skin at the last minute. Who knows what reserves of spirit lie hidden under the surface? Now that I am older I think somewhat differently about all of it. I have more sympathy for Faye, of course, and also more curiosity about where their marriage started from, what they ever liked in each other. And we all thought of their tale as over once Abe walked out, but it must've gone on—until both their deaths, I would say. People trim their stories too short, I've come to think.

I always thought about Abe and Faye when I considered leaving my husband. I had thoughts about this for so long it seemed like another of those plans people hang on to like hobbies, the trip to China they never take, the house in the country they never buy.

Terry, my husband, is sixty-eight years old. I am twenty years younger than he is, which has always made me think of myself as a bouncy girlish creature. There are worse illusions. I go to the gym; I've kept myself slender and peppy. Terry, who has never seen the inside of a gym and has drunk like a fish his entire adult life, looks remarkably good—his eyes have a pouchy but sly look, and his wrecked features are relaxed and hearty.

His constitution seems to hold up fine under a constant internal bath of alcohol. He has a lower cholesterol count than I do, and his blood pressure is quite medium. He shows every sign of being destined to live to a pickled hundred and ten. It used to make me angry that he got off so lightly, that he'd walked through a life of getting sodden every night without paying the price that most people pay.

On the other hand, I had reason to think I might turn out to be the price. As Terry sort of knew. "Would you like another cognac," he'd say, "to remember me by?" "Might as well eat that last piece of cake," he would say. "You'll miss it when you're gone."

So where did I think I was going? Although I'd had affairs, no one was waiting for me. I thought about living in Europe. Terry and I had once spent a year in Greece, and the college where I taught painting had programs in Paris and Florence. I had a friend who once worked for a company in Japan, and another friend whose eighty-year-old mother went to teach English in Poland. It's a big world, isn't it? The choices had to be numberless, once I opened the box.

But I liked many things about the life I had. I liked the rhythm of my week, the days in the studio against the days with students. I had a decent gallery. I had friends I'd had for twenty years. I was settled.

I had a long attachment to the place where we lived—a floor-through loft with high ceilings and tall windows. When I first came to New York, places like this were still findable. It had a rent no one could believe later, and it was illegal for living, zoned for commerce only. I had to keep my name off the buzzer, take my garbage to the corner, hook my electric lines into the hall light. I liked to do my paintings by floodlight, and I was always blowing a fuse if I forgot to unplug something before I made toast. The neighbors hated it when the hallways went dark because of me.

It got so I left a flashlight out for them on the first landing, just in case. One night an English guy who was staying with someone upstairs insisted on coming in to teach me how to make toast under the gas flame of the broiler. "You don't know a flipping thing, do you?" he said, in a friendly way. This was Terry and he's still like that. I said something like, "Oh, yeah, buddy, that's what you think," and smiled. He held a slice of toast to my lips, and I nibbled at it. Terry the successful older painter, me in a little knotted T-shirt and cutoffs: you get the picture.

He had been staying upstairs for months, and his host was not disappointed when he moved in with me. Right from the first, Terry took to New York. It was like a wild border town to him—bars open till four, the streets thronged with all types commingling, all desires honored at all hours. When he got drunk, his accent thickened so I couldn't understand him. "Get the wax out of your ears, woman!" he'd say. Once I spilled maple syrup on a drawing of his, but it was just nervousness from having him around so much. He did another drawing and called it "All Art Is Pancakes to Stefanie" (my name is spelled Stephanie). He was not interested when I talked about friends of mine and sometimes our dinner table conversation ran aground. I waited until he was out of the house and put on the records I liked. Once an old boyfriend came over and we had a quickie reunion on the sofa. Terry never found out, but I felt so bad about it I bought him a tiny jar of caviar, a favorite snack. "Why are you so good to me, my love?" he said. We had a picnic on the pier, with the skyline of New Jersey like a stage set.

We got married five weeks after Terry moved in. He needed his green card, and neither of us saw why I couldn't do him that favor. His friend upstairs was the witness. We didn't even tell people beforehand: what was there to tell? We had been living together and we were going to go on living together. We had both lived with people before. "Except for the blood test," I said, "this is painless."

Of course that wasn't quite right. I remember waiting in line in the municipal building, in a room filled with rows of folding chairs, and thinking, *Is this it? What is it?* People near us held bouquets and laughed to each other, an official handed out pamphlets, Terry stroked my thigh. I didn't want to be there. "*I Married an Alien*," I kept saying. I was in love with a certain kind of jolly irony, in those days. We had to wait an hour in that room. Somebody's mother, all decked out in yellow chiffon, said, "This is the happiest room in the city, right?" John, our witness, did coin tricks for somebody's three-year-old. Flashbulbs kept going off right near us. When the couple ahead of us was suddenly called in, I gave out a shriek. "Easy, girl," John said.

Terry said, "Don't faint on me. I'll have to marry John instead."

The Justice who intoned our ceremony said the words without any frills like enunciation or feeling, but they made my heart ache all the same. I had to repeat the vow (one sentence, taking as my husband) as if I meant it. Terry looked sobered and manly; perhaps he was more earnest than I was, underneath it all, or just then grateful. We were still in a hug when the Justice held the door open for us to leave.

The couple behind us—two sweet-faced people from the Philippines—hadn't known they would need a witness, and John ended up filling in for them too. The bride had me take their picture with John afterward; he smiled like a happy uncle. "Better wishes always," the bride said to me.

I wore an antique-lace blouse and jeans. We took a cab across town to a fancy restaurant for lunch, but they wouldn't let us in because of my pants. I hadn't thought ahead at all; I doubt that I'd really pictured any of it. We went to the bar we always went to—this was fine with me. As the afternoon went on, people we knew kept coming over to us and saying, "Is it true?" ("Not a word of it," Terry said, "all rumor and innuendo") and buying us drinks. Sometime in midevening we went home and took a nice, sexy nap, although we faded out before what you might call the consummation. I woke up in the middle of the night, dazed and headachy. I was still making jokes about the whole thing in my head. Terence who? I do what? I was saving up phrases for the story of it, to tell later to people like my second husband.

We were quarrelsome in the weeks after the wedding. Terry had—still has—the habit of holding forth, of airing his opinions without quarter. On his side, he hated the way I was always talking about him on the phone to my friends; he was not fooled by code names. All the same we both got caught up in making improvements on the loft—we had some hippie electrician rig up a better electric line, we partitioned studios for both of us, and in the bathroom (where I had been bathing one part at a time in an industrial sink) we brought in an old oil drum to use for a tub. You climbed a ladder over the side and sat on a stool under a hose, like a swimmer under a waterfall. We were quite proud of having devised this. We painted it with Rustoleum, and Terry put plants around it. Twenty years later it was still our bathtub. I'd had no idea.

TERRY ALMOST LEFT, years ago, with someone even younger than I was, but then he didn't. Now he's too old to go anywhere. His conversation is the same as it's always been—literally the same, I know these stories—except that he's more blustery, more like an old Brit. His voice is thicker and scratchier, and he gets winded on long walks. We walk around the city a lot, still.

This summer, on a walk to a friend's house, we ran into the woman Terry almost ran off with. Dahlia, her name is; that part is not her fault. I don't think she's aged well, but I wouldn't, would I? She is scrawny and jowly; I wouldn't wear a long tube dress if I were her. "Hello, hello," she said when she saw us. "I was just thinking about you because they had Tony Blair on the news. He's much better-looking than our politicians, don't you think?"

"The fun politician was John Major. His parents were circus people," Terry said. "Only man in history to run away from the circus to become an accountant." This wasn't a new one to me, but I saw

Dahlia grinning away, flashing her teeth. Terry went on at length about the Euro Market, and Dahlia showed many animated expressions in response. It alarmed me to see her. Not because I feared her effect on Terry—he would have a swelled head for the rest of the evening, that was all—but because I saw how I might turn out like her, if I left Terry. I could become an eager nodder, bubbling over with appreciation, so lit up by male conversation I could only make wild faces in reply. I could peer up and squint and stretch my skin in a beaming grimace.

Oh, maybe Dahlia was just nervous. Who knows how to act with an old flame and his spouse? Perhaps her usual life is quite wonderful. In the fluster of getting away from us, she actually kissed me goodbye on the lips.

Terry talked to me about scandals among the Tories for a good twenty blocks. "Why are you walking so fast?" he said. He was in the middle of the story about the cross-dressing MP who dropped dead in a men's room, fishnet stockings and all. "You look like a duck when you walk that way," he told me.

Terry was just warming up when we got to our friends' for dinner. "Did you know John Major's parents were in the circus?" he said as they opened the door. We were eating with our old neighbor, John, and his second wife, Susan. Their five-year-old, Max, was on the floor building something out of Legos. They got to hear about the cross-dressing M.P. who dropped dead in a men's room.

"Know what Max did yesterday?" John said. "Tell them, buddy. He had his first swim class, and he could do the dead man's float *without* a kickboard. He got into it right away."

I like the way John is now. I like these gung-ho old-guy fathers.

I bent down to take a look at what Max was building, something between a skyscraper and a dinosaur. "If you stick your bum out like that," Terry told me, "someone's going to smack it." John and Susan may have thought this was a little marital joke about precoital spanking, but it was just hostility. I kept my bum stuck out, for spite.

Terry came over to check out the Lego project himself. "Hey! What are you doing?" Max said.

"You need an expert to show you how it's done," Terry said.

"He doesn't," I said.

Terry was adding on some sort of flying buttress. Max wailed like a siren.

"It looks better now," Terry said. "See that? It's much better. Ask anyone. They know great art when they see it."

It is possible that if Terry and I had had a child, Terry wouldn't be so boxed in now, so caught up in doing the same few things he knows. When we first got married, some people did ask if I was pregnant, that being the first guess about a sudden marriage. We both expressed some hilarity at the thought. Not that, not us. I was probably waiting (no rush) for someone to have a child with.

"I know a boy who's tired," Susan said to Max. "A boy whose bedtime may be somewhere in the very near future."

"And then I'll have the Legos all to myself," Terry said. This was not a joke Max liked. He screamed again. Terry waved a Lego block at him.

Max was bribed with a dish of ice cream in the kitchen, allowed to watch a video, and finally led off to bed by John. From the living room we could hear his bedtime music, the Backstreet Boys and 'N Sync.

Terry sang along; he likes to sing when he's been drinking. He didn't know any of the words. Dooby dooby dooby, he sang. I was thinking: if he had gone off with Dahlia, my life would've been different and better.

Dahlia in those days was quite formidable, with a vibrant if somewhat hysterical style. Terry must have kept her dangling for a long while. What arrogance on his part, I thought. I felt quite sullen about all of it, and mopey with longing.

When John came back, and the roast chicken with pine nuts was brought out, the whole time I was munching and drinking and half-listening to all of them, I was musing about leaving Terry. It wasn't so different from when I was a college girl and I'd be having lustful fantasies about some boy, in the middle of a holiday dinner at home. Perhaps my family guessed, from my expression; perhaps Susan and John guessed something now. They let me sit without talking, although I am usually quite chatty.

At the end of the night I got Terry into a cab, although he tried to insist on walking. Within about a minute, he was slumped against me, almost asleep but not quite. He kissed my shoulder wetly. "My sweet guy," I said. I was false by habit; that was the worst part.

The next day I got up and bought the newspapers and came back and made us pancakes for breakfast. Terry can eat even with a hangover; perhaps this is the secret of his health. The wifely meal was a kind of lie too on my part, all that solicitous offering of hot sausages and cooling orange juice. Terry was blustering about how spoiled Max was. I was reading the back of the paper, the ads for Lofts for Rent, Lofts for Sale. Sunny floor-thru, windows on all sides, a steal for the right renter. Even in Brooklyn and Jersey City nothing was cheap, and everything was through brokers now. *Gd blk, oldr bldg, lng lease.*

I was dead serious, but it wasn't going to be any snap to begin again. In a movie a character moves into an empty apartment and in the next scene it's transformed into a complete dwelling, furnished and filled out. In real life, many a room lies bare for lack of hope and will. I knew that.

But the ads themselves, column after column, were kernels of optimism, little vistas curled up into captions. I had an income of sorts from my teaching job, and I was not a sissy about neighborhoods. I wasn't young, but I was appreciably younger than my uncle Abe was when he cut loose. He must have waited until he couldn't stand it one second longer; I felt superior to Abe, from having more years left.

Terry thought I was reading my horoscope in the paper. (He was a great scoffer at astrology—he missed Nancy Reagan still.) "Opportunity is knocking on my door and a new adventure may surprise my friends," I said. It pleased me to fool him, more than a little; this is a pleasure people don't talk about.

I kissed Terry on the elbow when I got up. "Hi, hot stuff," I said. "My girl," he said. Then I went for a walk, and from the pay phone on our corner I called one of the brokers in Brooklyn. The line was busy and I had to call back over and over, while an irritated bike messenger waited to use the phone. A woman finally answered, keyed up and loud from talking to everyone else. Yes! I could see it! Today! Lots of people were calling! Three o'clock!

Terry had gone to bed again when I got back to the loft. I went into my studio to try to paint but I couldn't. I was too happy. After all these years, my erroneous, inadvertent life was about to turn into a clean slate, a blank page: start here. From happiness I went out again just to walk. The streets were glowing with daylight, everything was sun and chrome. I was delirious. I bought a copy of the same paper I had at home, and I walked ten blocks until I found a phone that worked and called two more brokers. I made appointments for the next day and for later in the week. It wasn't hard.

I went to my art supply store and spent three hundred twenty-two dollars on things I'd needed for a while and now decided I deserved. I knew it was a sign of manic frenzy, this shopping, but I don't do it often and I believe I should do it more. Life is short, is what I was thinking. Go. Do it now.

It is hard to describe what I felt, carrying home the packages and walking up my own stairs after this. I felt sentimental, as if I were visiting my old grammar school. The warped steps and the peeling banister looked ancient and discarded. I felt pleasantly guilty and elated with refusal, as if I had just turned away a regiment of pleading suitors.

Terry didn't come to the door when I unlocked it, and he wasn't in the bedroom when I looked. What was I planning to do? Give him a massage, a feast of fake attentions, a last duplicitous fuck? In any case, he was in his studio or he was out. I took all the new art supplies to my own studio, and I unpacked them and looked them over, gloating, and then I packed them up again, for the move.

When I went into the bathroom before the subway ride, I saw that some of the plants had been knocked over. The clay pot holding a big palm near the window was shattered—dirt and fronds were on the floor. The sight of this scared me, and I thought I heard something, a single hoarse note. For a minute I didn't do anything but stand still, as if I were in the woods trying not to make noise.

On the floor, behind the oil drum of the tub, a bare male leg was stretched out—a pale veinous leg with dark hairs. I screamed when I saw that.

And then I saw the rest of it, Terry's body, splayed out and crumpled, on the bath rug. His head was slumped to one side, and his hair was still wet from the shower. His eyes were open, and he was looking at me, in terror and mortification. He was making that frail moaning sound. I put a towel over him—I thought he might be in shock—and I said things like *I'm here, what happened, it's okay now.* When

I put my hand on his forehead, I couldn't tell if his skin was warm; I couldn't tell anything. He looked so piteous and imploring, an old man washed ashore. There was a bloody gash over his eye, and he was lying where he must have skidded into the plants after trying to climb out of that joke of a tub. That tub.

I did what had to be done, which was simple enough: I went to the phone and called for help. It was one of the first simple things in my wedded life. While I stood by Terry and waited for the ambulance, a look passed between us of shared astonishment, but I suppose we have been surprised by everything.

TERRY WAS NOT A GOOD PATIENT. He had been, as the doctor said, stunned, and he had a concussion (nothing else) and had to be kept under observation for a week. He was speaking again within hours, and the first thing he said was, "Who is that ugly woman?" meaning the doctor. I thought he meant me—I was wild with gladness that he was talking, and at the same time I was furious and hurt. The doctor, an ordinary-looking woman with a slight mustache, asked if he knew who the Vice President was, a test he passed. The next time I came in Terry was advising the orderly on the right way to mop. At the end of the week he was judged fine, no major damage, ready to go home for good.

The day we came home from the hospital, I held his arm when we went up the stairs, and I thought we had crossed over the line to his really being old. It was a gray day and the big space of the loft looked drab. The plumbers were spending a long time putting in the new tub, and until they finished we had to take cat-baths over the sink, the way we used to. Terry had bruises and a Band-Aid above one eye, like an old bum, and he cursed and sputtered while he stood naked splashing himself. I helped him wash the parts he was too sore to reach.

He got me to wait on him, as I might've known he would. He had me run out for things he suddenly wanted—an art magazine, a detective novel he wasn't really going to read—and he had me bring him snacks in his studio—soup or grilled cheese, food it took a little time to make. I didn't mind; in his place I might've done the same.

It was the evenings, after dinner, when he told the same unbearable stories over again, that made me sorry for myself. The time he climbed Mount Snowdon in the rain, what the actress said to him at his first opening. I never hated Terry, for all that we held against each other, but we were never wholehearted as a couple, and it weighed on me now that I had missed that.

I should have paid attention, I shouldn't have been so easy about everything; I might have had a more honest life. I have to know that, at the same time that I don't now imagine ever leaving this husband or this house. Not anymore; a fact is a fact. It is the first time I've been so resolute. At the art school where I teach, everyone tells me how calm I am these days.

Terry has mellowed some, since his accident. His drinking is less boisterous, more in the Mediterranean tradition of the old men who sit around the square half-stewed all day. He paints in the morning—his painting is not going badly—and then he sips his way through the better part of the afternoon. When I come out of my studio, he is often napping in his chair, and he wakes up, with his hair sticking up in tufts and his glasses on crooked, and he pinches my behind as I go by, although I have told him for years not to.

I don't get as angry with him as I once did. I seem to have passed out of most of that during those moments when I believed he was going to die, although, in his Terry way, he fooled us both. This time. Since his return home, he hovers over me quite a lot—he watches me in the kitchen, he gets underfoot when I'm vacuuming—and he has developed a new concern with my health. Am I sneezing or sweating or limping? I happen to be fine. He wants to remind me I am not different from him, which of course I am not; I do know that. I can't help knowing. This isn't the easiest or the softest or the best part of my life, but the simplest things are clearer to me now.

Commendable

Marcia's parents, who were still in New Jersey, were truly happy when she came to live in the East again. Her father said, "Hey! That's more like it," when she first told them she was moving to New York. "About time!" her mother said. Nobody mentioned the years when they had been so bitterly against her. Her parents were old now, and the fights were over long since. What had they fought about? Sex, Marcia would say. Sex in various forms. And who had asked them to be so nosy? Marcia had lived with some men who were not great people, she had danced in a topless club, she had been in one dirty movie that very few people saw—but it had never been her idea to share this news or to try to make it intelligible to them. Her poor parents, how raging and mean they had been. The whole thing had been one spell of time for Marcia, among many, and not the most regrettable. For years now she'd been a regular person who worked at a job, and her parents said,

"Sweetheart, you are so gorgeous," when they saw her, and, "Don't be a stranger," when she left.

Now that Marcia was living nearby, she could see that her parents had changed quite a lot. They had once been sociable people, bridge players and party givers, but now they hardly went out. Her father was convinced that the teenage boy next door was casing the house when he walked around in his own backyard, and her mother believed that someone was stealing gravel from their driveway. They gave their dire reports with foxy satisfaction—oh, they knew what was going on, they were well aware. "It's a different world," they said, correctly, although its difference made them read it wrong, Marcia thought.

They were still in the same house where Marcia had grown up, a roomy colonial that got good sun. And the town seemed remarkably the same, Marcia decided, when she came for a weekend and was sent out to shop. Mitchell's Hardware was still there, only with a new sign, and Garfield's Fine Footwear was in the same spot on Franklin Avenue. Even the shoes in the window looked eternal—patent leather Mary Janes for girls, brown Oxfords for men, pointy pumps for women.

On the other hand, where the Sweet Shoppe had been was a store that sold exercise equipment, and next door was a Caffe delle Quattro Stagioni, which smelled deliciously of espresso. The Caffe was all chrome and tile, sleekly authentic, but the woman coming out the door, as Marcia went by, could have been one of the mothers from her youth. She had a look of breezy competence that Marcia had almost forgotten about, a modest but sturdy expression; she wore a blouse and Bermuda shorts, and her hair was in a short, tidy cut (like a little cap, Marcia's mother would have said). "Hello, hello," the woman said. "What are you doing here?" She was definitely speaking to Marcia.

"Visiting the old homestead," Marcia said. "How are you?" She had no idea, not a clue.

The woman chuckled, a little spitefully, and said, "You don't know me, do you?" but from that dark chuckle Marcia did know. It was Kaye Brightley, older sister of Ivy, who had been Marcia's best friend in junior high.

What was Kaye doing here? She lived here, had always lived here. She had a job at the pharmaceutical company on the highway, and she had her own house out by where Heiling's Ice Cream used to be. "How's Ivy?" Marcia said.

"In London still. She likes it. You know she's divorced? Her kids are fine, they're old now. She's good. She's living with someone. How are *you* doing?"

Marcia said she was just now on her way to buy tomato plants for her mother.

"I wouldn't get them at Mitchell's if I were you," Kaye said. "The good place is the nursery in East Brook. That's where Jimmy gets his, and he has an amazing garden."

"Jimmy McPhaill?" Marcia said.

Was nothing changed here at all? Jimmy had been Kaye's constant companion all through high school. For a while they'd had a romance (of some kind, Ivy and Marcia had done a lot of wild guessing about what kind) but this had fallen apart soon, and after a brief cooling-off period they'd gone back to being buddies. Marcia thought later that Jimmy was probably gay. An opera lover, a sports hater, an impassioned fan of Emily Dickinson. Although now when she thought of him he seemed corny and avuncular and hearty, someone whose jokes would be all wrong in most gay circles.

She and Ivy, the young pests, had hung around Jimmy as much as he would let them, pale and unhandsome though he was. He had been quite nice to them. He lent them books and made them listen to Gilbert and Sullivan. He took them out for sundaes, with Kaye, and acted tickled by their greed for chocolate, their crushes on the counter guy. Marcia and Ivy were goofy, feverish creatures then; by the time they were more composed, he was gone. Kaye was always shooing them away—"Hey, kidlets, go take a short walk off a long pier"—but she put up with them better than most older sisters would have.

"He's a stupendous gardener," Kaye said. "Every square inch of his yard, back and front, has something sprouting out of it. Every year there's more."

"Say what you will," Marcia groaned, "New York does not have real vegetation. They chain down the saplings."

Marcia went on so long about New York's pathetic, scraggly ginko trees that before she knew it she was agreeing to go see Jimmy's place. "He can tell you everything you need to know about tomatoes," Kaye said. "He's the one who knows. And then you can get a quick view of the garden, which you really have to see."

Marcia followed Kaye's car out of the town's old center, onto a road with a mall of newer stores, into the hillier, wealthier, more countrified expanses where Jimmy's parents had always lived. The parents were both dead by now, Marcia had just been told, and he was in their house alone.

Even from a distance you could see that the grounds of Jimmy's house were like nothing else around them. Marcia's first impression was of an illustration from a Victorian children's book, with roses on trellises and sweet peas clinging by their tendrils to a fence. Everything seemed lush and innocent. And that was only the side of the house. When they parked in the back, they walked out into something more formal and rhythmic—beds of red and pink and blue, trailing arches of lavender and white, and even a sculpted bramble in the shape of a spire. Marcia, who did not know the names of many flowers, was dazzled by the cunning, intricate shapes, the bell-shaped cups and the open, flat blooms, big as cymbals, and the cascades of frothy white bushes. Sitting on a bench was a large person in a striped shirt and khakis who was Jimmy.

"I didn't know you were coming!" he said to Kaye, when he got up to greet her. He was better-looking as a grown-up, more evenly proportioned. He'd become a broad-faced man with a beard, quite substantial. Still a little soft around the edges maybe. When Marcia was explained to him, he said, "Well, well, well."

He thought she didn't like him; Marcia could see that. He thought she still found him clumsy and unimpressive. Once, when he was home from college, he had taken her out for ice cream, and she had acted quite superior with him then. Marcia had forgotten all about this part of it.

Kaye made Jimmy give a tour of every petal and leaf in the garden, which Marcia was genuinely thrilled by. "What do you think?" Kaye said. "Unbelievable, right?"

"You're amazing," Marcia told Jimmy. "I'm amazed. This is too much, this place."

"Right," he said.

"This is a whole kingdom here. You must work your fingers to the bone, just to get the tea roses like that. Roses and more roses."

Marcia was gushing, but he was hard to talk to, and it was often her instinct to flatter men. She supposed she wanted to stop this; maybe not.

"I've never seen a private garden as incredible as this."

"Shucks," he said.

"No, really."

"I could show you the potting shed," he said. "That's what makes it easier, that I had that built here. The hideaway."

"She doesn't want to see that ratty piece of architecture," Kaye said. "Let her sit down."

Uh-oh. Marcia sat down, just in case Kaye thought she was after Jimmy.

"Do you like root beer?" Kaye asked. Jimmy was sent inside to bring them some.

"This place *is* incredible," Marcia said, one more time.

"Every night when I come over, he's playing in the dirt," Kaye said. "He wouldn't do vegetables for a long time, but I talked him into it."

Jimmy was back with the root beer in glass mugs. "The Kaye does not believe in ice cubes for this beverage."

If they weren't a couple, they managed to sound like one. And they matched: the primly casual clothes, the streaks of gray in their hair. But perhaps they were both thinking that Marcia looked foolishly juvenile with her bleached ponytail and her short sundress. They wanted to hear about whatever she'd been up to. A long story. Marcia stuck to the here and now. She had a little, little apartment in New York—the size of a gym locker—and she was a program counselor at Planned Parenthood.

"I see a lot of teenage girls," she said. "You would not believe some of the outfits. They're a cute group. Quite hip. We didn't know about getting our own birth control at that age."

"Speak for yourself," Kaye said.

"Why, Kaye," Marcia said.

"I mean boys knew to buy condoms. Another idea that's come around again."

"Car fins are next," Jimmy said.

"We didn't have the risks," Kaye said, "that they have now."

Had Kaye had sex in high school? Marcia had never imagined her doing any such thing—Kaye with her boxy body, her flat voice. When things got wild in America, Kaye was already out of school. Marcia, who was only five years younger, thought of herself as from another generation, on the boat Kaye had just missed. But who knew what Kaye had been up to? Perhaps she and Jimmy had ventured into those waters, and then turned back.

"Condoms aren't the only things we send people out with," Marcia said. "It depends."

"Better than having them on welfare, right, Jimmy?" Kaye said.

"I'm not against freedom for anybody," Jimmy said. "I just wish they had husbands so the taxpayers wouldn't have to marry them."

"Those stubborn girls," Marcia said, "turning away those eager husbands."

They probably thought she sounded bitter, which she was not, or not about those things; heartless desertions hadn't been her problem. She liked men still, she still cooed and trilled around them, and when would this end? She hoped before it became ridiculous.

Jimmy said, "Okay, blame the boys. Go ahead." On that last trip out for a sundae with Jimmy, she remembered now, he had turned caustic when she'd said she was going to be very, very busy the next few days. "Thank you for your time this afternoon," he had said. She had not told Kaye about any of it.

"Jimmy gets stuck on one theory," Kaye said. "Who could believe that husbands are the answer?"

"I couldn't, personally," Marcia said. "I've had three. One of them isn't quite done yet. You ever have one?"

"Not me," Kaye said.

"Me neither," Jimmy said.

"I got to see things, at least, because of them," Marcia said. "I lived in Mexico, and before that I was in Senegal for a while."

"I've only been to England," Kaye said. "To see Ivy."

"Where I'd like to go someday is Japan," Jimmy said. "I'd be interested to see the gardens."

"Me, too," Kaye said. Jimmy had money. What was stopping them?

"Asia," Jimmy said, "is great for games." He went and got his mahjong set to show Marcia. The tiles were antique ivory. Marcia said the set was beautiful, but she begged off on joining their tournament, which had been running for years, according to the score sheets. Actually in Mexico, where she'd had a lot of leisure, Marcia had been quite a passable mahjong player.

By the time Marcia got advice about the tomato plants, she decided it was too late to drive over to buy them in East Brook. When she called home to explain where she was, her mother didn't seem to mind. "I've been hanging out with Kaye Brightley and her boyfriend," Marcia said. "Remember Ivy? Kaye's the sister."

"I know who she is, she's been around here for years. Boyfriend who?" Marcia's mother said. "I thought she liked girls."

IT WAS MARCIA'S FIRST SUMMER in the East in many years, and she had underestimated how hot New York could get. The wiring in her building was too old for air conditioners. She tooks dips in the municipal pool on Carmine Street, remnant of a nobler civic vision and safe even now, but so crowded it was like swimming on the subway. As a child, she had swum in Russell Pond in Russell Park, a few blocks from her house. The pond's bottom was as muddy as ever, she found out one weekend. The water was warm and smelled like tadpoles. Local children were surprised to see her there; adults almost never went in, and most of the morning you had to be a kid taking a class to use it. Several times Marcia swam there in the late afternoon, when the light was bright and dappled.

Neither Kaye nor Jimmy would go with her. Too public, and Kaye had once seen a leech in the water. (So had Marcia, but not lately.) But whenever she could, Marcia stopped in at Jimmy's garden before she went home and had gin and tonics with the two them; the root beer, it turned out, was only for before three. "Greetings, thirsty voyager," Jimmy would say. Marcia was still stumped on the question of whether or not they were a couple. They seemed to spend together every minute that Kaye wasn't working. (Jimmy lived off what he referred to as family holdings and apparently had quite an open schedule.) They went out for movies and dinners and drives to the country, and their conversation was as full of old stories and minor bickering as any couple's. Marcia had never seen them embrace, but they were Episcopalians, as Marcia's mother liked to point out, and not young. But then why did they live separately? Why wouldn't they marry? Kaye's house—small and ugly, in a new development—was bare and provisional inside, as if she were waiting to see about it, although she had lived there for years.

On weekends Kaye did go off without Jimmy for a few hours, to play basketball with a group of women, and it was this—and her square-torsoed, no-nonsense sturdiness—that had given Marcia's mother her ideas about Kaye's sexual preference. "And her manner," Marcia's mother said. She found Kaye gruff and unaccommodating. "A person who is not trying to be pleasant."

"Mother," Marcia said. "Nobody goes through the day being girly and sugary any more. Kaye has a responsible job. She wears a suit and bosses people around."

"I heard. She makes a nice living," Marcia's mother said.

"They all have to now," Marcia's father said. "Am I right?"

Marcia could not imagine Kaye having sex with another woman (something she had watched in person, in fact, more than once), but she knew that watching was unnatural and so anyone was almost impossible to picture swept away in the mechanics. Marcia herself had never much liked mirrors; she liked to close her eyes. So perhaps Kaye had known unspeakable splendors. Jimmy was a whole other set of secrets.

Neither of them seemed at all miserable. Kaye liked her job, as far as Marcia could see. She talked about it with a possessive irritation, a pride in its vexations, always, Marcia thought, a sign of love. She complained about how she always had to check every single thing her "people" did without making them feel like nincompoops. She was probably good at all this.

One night Kaye telephoned Marcia at home for advice about what to wear to a company awards banquet. "A swank affair," she said. She must have been to this kind of thing before, but she probably knew that her type—the dowdy woman of integrity—wasn't what was wanted for corporate display; she was a respected throwback. "Dark red silk would be good with your coloring," Marcia said. "Spend money." But they both knew Kaye would look like Kaye anyway.

Otherwise they never spoke to each other outside Marcia's visits. Neither Kaye nor Jimmy showed the slightest interest in setting foot on the island of Manhattan. Marcia could go for a few weeks without thinking about either of them. Her job was busy and packed with other people's crises, and at night she had long, ill-advised phone conversations with Alejandro, the man she had left her husband Mike for, and also with Mike, who was now living with a twenty-four-year-old but was balking about the divorce.

Marcia was glad for her solitude, with its peace and freedom, but she was sorry she was never going to sleep with either Mike or Alejandro again. And perhaps with no one else either; she knew lots of people—men and women both, her age and other ages—who did without. She could see the advantages, but she had lived a good part of her life trying to be faithful to the currents of desire, sworn to that if to nothing else. At nineteen, in the topless bar, prancing around on that catwalk stage, she'd thought she was dancing out the most urgent truth, repeating what everyone knew, only more prettily, with her smudged eyes and her rouged breasts; what a vain girl she had been and how caught up in one single idea. Even later, when she couldn't stand to be anywhere near the Carnival Club, nothing had seemed clearer to her than the primacy of sexual feeling. But maybe her own fate was that she had passed now into another stage, another state. She could imagine it, or almost. But she would have to move to another line of work, where she wasn't all the time explaining to teenagers where their cervixes were.

In a general way, she was fine now, with her tiny apartment, her ambling routines, her touristy pleasure in the noise and sociability of the New York streets. She had a few old friends here from other places, and a few cronies at work whom she liked. In autumn the weather was clear and pleasant. Manhattan (she told Alejandro) was a handsome city, garbage and all.

In the brightest part of October, Kaye called to ask if Marcia wanted to come spend a weekend with them in the country, in a house Jimmy's father had owned, near the Delaware Water Gap. Another relative used it in the summer, but Jimmy wouldn't leave his garden then and Kaye said they liked it in the fall. "Come be a leaf-peeper," Kaye said. "We don't do anything more strenuous than that, I promise."

"You always missed the autumns in the East," Mike said, when she told him she was going.

On Saturday morning she took the train to New Jersey, where Kaye and Jimmy met her at the station, and they rode over highways whose bordering trees were suddenly blazing with color. All that miraculous color, the backlit leaves glowing against the sky, made Marcia fiercely homesick for Alejandro and for Mike, for things over and done with.

The house, which had been quite isolated when he was a kid, Jimmy said, was on a road now dotted with new chalets and A-frames. In the afternoon, joggers of all ages went past and waved to the three of them on the porch; they sat sipping bourbon and sodas, Kaye's drink of choice for the season. The hillside behind them was dazzling.

At dusk they went inside and Kaye brought out a Scrabble set. "Don't let Jimmy try his fake words. He's ruthless," she said. They were clever players, both of them, good at placing their letters on the high-scoring squares and reusing *Q*'s and *X*'s. Marcia was beaten badly. "The Kaye is unstoppable tonight," Jimmy said.

In the kitchen, Kaye stood at the stove, with a bib apron over her wool slacks, and made them what she called a lazy dinner, chicken baked in some sort of salad dressing, not bad. "Children," she said, "you may pick up your drumsticks. We're in the country."

Would Kaye have made a good mother? You could say she had the life of a suburban matron, without the family to go with it. Had she been cheated of her best fate, or would she have been one of those sour, hotly resigned mothers of Marcia's childhood? If Kaye mourned the road not taken, it didn't show. She did have Jimmy, who at the moment was gnawing away intently at his bone. "You can't get a better bird than this," he said. "Not if you shot it yourself." They were three middle-aged adults without children, although Marcia had at least done things you wouldn't want kids along for. Not that anyone was handing out medals for that.

"In Senegal the chicken, when you got any, was as tough as shoe leather," Marcia said. "At dinners, conversations would hit these long pauses while people were chewing." She noticed she wanted to brag about herself, where she had been and with whom.

"I'd like to go to Africa," Jimmy said.

"He doesn't even have a passport," Kaye said.

"Actually, mine is expired too," Marcia said.

"Really?" Kaye said. "This shocks me, about you."

"Oh, boy," Marcia said. "My current life would shock you then. I don't do a thing."

"What qualifies as a thing?" Jimmy said.

"Don't ask," Marcia said. He looked sly and laughed his old laugh, a hawing guffaw. Marcia felt very racy, not happily. It might be harder than she'd thought, spending a whole weekend with the two of them.

But then Kaye brought out the dessert—do-it-yourself sundaes, with fudge sauce and Redi-wip and shredded coconut and a jar of walnuts in syrup. "You don't do this all the time, do you?" Marcia said.

"Sure we do," Kaye said.

"Sundae comes once a week," Jimmy said. "Isn't that the idea?"

"I'm in heaven," Marcia said.

WHERE WERE JIMMY AND KAYE planning to sleep? That was the question. Marcia's own suitcase had been taken to a dark corner room with sloped eaves, charming in a gloomy way, across the hall from the master bedroom, whose open door showed that somebody's method of unpacking was to dump all the stuff on the floor. When they all went upstairs to bed, Jimmy went into this room, and Kaye stood in the hall saying, "Sweet dreams," and then she went into another bedroom, next door to Marcia's. That's it then, Marcia thought, I should have known.

Marcia was probably glad, more or less. Lying in the single bed, under a weighty mound of wool blankets, she liked to think of all three of them, tucked up in their separate realms, cozy enough. Like children, or like commendable old people in a British novel. To each his own, she thought.

But in the middle of the night Marcia was awakened by a single, soft cry. From Jimmy's room she could hear gasping and short, quick breaths. Ah, well, she thought, let them, but she felt like a man in the audience at the Carnival Club, trapped in his own rapt attention, dumb and hooked and mocked. (*Who doesn't want to watch?* the owner had said. *What else is interesting?*) Then Marcia heard Kaye calling, "Jimmy, Jimmy," but the voice came from next door, from Kaye's own room. The door opened, and Kaye ran out into the hall.

It was not sex—what was wrong with Marcia, that that was all she knew about?—it was a medical crisis or a bad dream. Marcia was probably not wanted in the second case, and she lay still for a minute—Jimmy's voice, a low monotone, seemed to be reassuring Kaye—and then she got up any way. How could she pretend not to have heard? Wasn't she here in the house with them? Kaye turned on the light just as Marcia stood in the doorway, and there was Jimmy sitting up in bed, red-faced and sweating; he looked as if he'd been boiled. His hair and his beard were as wet as a swimmer's.

"Are you all right?" Marcia said.

"I woke you up," Jimmy said. "We should've put you downstairs."

"He has medicine he takes," Kaye said. "Don't worry about it. Go back to bed."

"Sorry," Marcia said, and got out of there.

Oh, Jimmy, she thought, back in her room, you could have just told me. How long had he had night sweats? Kaye's face had been heavy with a tight, mournful anger. But they might've kept her away from the house overnight, if they really had wanted to keep all of this private and hidden.

Perhaps Marcia was not supposed to say anything about it to them. As if she didn't hand out pamphlets every day urging people to get tested in four languages. She wondered if Jimmy had a wild and separate nocturnal life with other men, or a longtime lover he just didn't tell people like her about. Jimmy acted as if he didn't know what year it was, Marcia thought, and yet he must know.

At breakfast Kaye was still angry, or plenty miffed, at any rate. "I tell him to just do the *basics* to take care of himself," she said. "It's the least he could do, don't you think? Does he get monitored by the doctor when he's supposed to? No. Does he exercise at all ever? No. Not him."

"He has to be careful. It can make a big difference," Marcia said. Jimmy, who was sitting right across from them spooning up his cereal, said, "He has to put up with everybody's free advice."

"What are they giving him?" Marcia said to Kaye.

"That's another thing," Kaye said. "Nitroglycerine pills dissolved on the tongue—that can't be the best they can do for angina. Really. Does that sound like a nineteenth-century treatment or what?"

"The heart," Jimmy said, "is a nineteenth-century organ. I have a quaint, outdated malady."

Marcia saw Jimmy's heart, a sequestered valentine, pulsing in its wine-velvet casing. Apparently she was never going to guess right about it.

"Your *father* took those little nitro pills," Kaye said. "How state-of-the-art can they be?"

Jimmy carried his bowl to the sink and walked out of the kitchen.

"None of my beeswax," Kaye said. "That's his way of letting me know."

"Is he all right?" Marcia said.

"He's not all right," Kaye said. "He knows he's not."

"You can't make him take care of himself if he won't."

"Who, then?" Kaye said. "Who else?"

Marcia was about to say, *He has to do it himself*, but that was just some California jive; perhaps it was her own jive.

"He just goes on in his merry, pigheaded way," Kaye said. "He leaves it to me to worry. I'm the one. It's my job." Kaye was washing the breakfast dishes as she spoke. Steam was rising from the sink.

She went at the counter with a sponge, scouring hard. "He just goes off. And you see how he leaves the kitchen. Look at this crud."

"You could ignore the crud," Marcia said. "That's kind of my philosophy."

"Yes," Kaye said. She went on rub-a-dub-dubbing.

"Do you do this whenever you come out here?" Marcia said. "Clean the house?"

"Well, I have to," Kaye said.

"Mike, my husband, was a great housekeeper," Marcia said. "I think I got neater because of him."

"Jimmy hasn't gotten neater," Kaye said. She was taking a broom out of a closet. Marcia followed her into the hallway, where she began sweeping.

"I'll do something," Marcia said. "Do you want me to do something?"

"You're the guest," Kaye said.

Kaye was raising a lot of dust, attacking the floor with great lunges of the broom. She seemed invigorated by her housework and her wifely griping. Marcia sat down to watch and felt left out.

Music came suddenly from the living room. A jolly tenor was telling them that he was the captain of the *Pinafore* and a right good captain too. "Ah," Kaye said. "He's put that on for me. He's sick of it but I still like it."

Jimmy came out of the living room then, doing a two-step to the chorus that was giving three cheers and one cheer more. If it was his way of ending their quarrel, it worked. Kaye knew the words to all the verses. Jimmy held the dustpan for her, and they bobbed around in time. "What movie are we in?" Marcia said.

After this Jimmy went out to get the Sunday paper, and when he came back, they all sat in the now dustless parlor and read through every section. Jimmy and Kaye muttered at the articles and read bits of news aloud every so often, and they did the crossword puzzle together, seated next to each other with rival pencils. What if sex were just taken out of the world? Marcia thought. Kaye and Jimmy were like an illustration from a book explaining how this could be done.

What would you do if you were blind? What if you couldn't walk? People always imagined how their senses got sharpened, their appreciations grew within a smaller focus; less stood in the way of their attentions; they became keen and sharp. Marcia was remembering all this.

"This puzzle was designed by a sadist rogue computer," Jimmy said.

"Anybody want to go for a walk?" Marcia said. "A little pre-lunch constitutional?"

"Jimmy sort of has to take it easy today," Kaye said. "Normally I encourage him to move his butt but now, no."

This meant that Kaye was not going either, and when Marcia took off for a quick stroll, the two of them waved to her from the porch. It was not Jimmy's fault he had to rest, but they were both so generally quiet in their habits, not to say pokey. Marcia always felt young and coltish next to them, but she wasn't so young, was she?

The weather was not as bright today—a white sky, a dampness in the air—and the foliage looked less fiery, but still panoramically terrific. Marcia went around gathering up the best leaves, the deepest reds and flashiest combos. She did this for something to do, but also with the idea of sending a few in the mail to Alejandro, who had never seen the leaves change color.

When she got back to the house, Jimmy was napping on the porch, and Kaye was inside reading a mystery and looking drowsy. Neither of them could have slept much the night before. Marcia showed Kaye her leaf assortment—"to send to a friend in California."

"Press them first," Kaye said.

Kaye didn't ask anything about the friend, which disappointed Marcia. She seemed to want to speak about him. "My friend Alejandro," she said. "Who's never been north of Marin County."

A flush of affection for Alejandro had crept over her on the leaf hunt. "My pen pal," she said, although really they were phone pals.

"I see," Kaye said. She did her knowing chuckle.

"He's a total Californian," Marcia said. "He's never been to New York."

"I've never been to the West Coast."

"It'll be his first visit. He's coming probably in the winter," Marcia said. "I like the idea of showing him the snow." Why was she saying this? She was making it up.

"Better tell him to bring a lot of layers to wear," Kaye said.

"I told him to wait till spring but he wants to come after Christmas." Marcia knew it was childish to lie like this but she couldn't stop. She didn't even *want* Alejandro to come, she was fairly sure. She watched Kaye's expression, which was mildly amused and a little put out that Marcia had been keeping secrets.

"It's so small in that apartment," Marcia said, "but we'll manage."

She couldn't help it, she felt better. "The man snores," she said, "and hogs all the room in the bed."

Over lunch, which was BLT sandwiches, Marcia said, "I used to cook more but I stopped."

"Better produce in California," Jimmy said.

"Alejandro likes to cook. It spoiled me. On camping trips even, we ate well," Marcia said. "You wouldn't believe I would go camping, would you?"

"There are trails around here," Kaye said. "Somewhere."

"We had good equipment. One of those dome tents, one of those amazing lightweight sleeping bags. It was Alejandro's stuff, actually."

Kaye looked amused again.

By late afternoon it was time to drive back. Kaye and Jimmy didn't like to drive at night. On the highway Marcia was afraid they were going to play one of those family car games—count all the signs with S in them, that sort of thing—but instead they listened to a tape of *The Mikado*. If you want to know who we are, we are gentlemen of Japan. Kaye insisted on driving, although Jimmy looked much better than he had in the morning."Alejandro drives like a nut," Marcia said. "He's good but he's too fast. It's hold-on-to-your-hat time when he's behind the wheel."

"That's California, isn't it?" Kaye said.

"Are you freezing?" Jimmy said to Kaye. "You look like you're freezing." He took off his cardigan and put it around her shoulders. It was one of those old man's sweaters, droopy and gray, and even from the back it made Kaye look like Margaret Rutherford. "Better? Okay?" Jimmy said. What scared Marcia was that she was starting to envy them.

"It's the way Alejandro takes the turns," Marcia said. "Too much."

She was making Alejandro sound pretty dashing. He was actually a fairly quiet person aside from his driving habits. She didn't think it was Alejandro she wanted to see, but he was the phantom object of desire now, the readiest emblem of plain and definite lust. Even now, Marcia thought she didn't really understand what life was without this, and she hoped she never knew, but in time it was likely she would. How little she had imagined before now, how slender her horizons had been.

"Campers," Kaye said. "I see a Dairy Queen ahead. What do you think?"

"Let our lovely guest decide," Jimmy said.

"Stop we must," Marcia said.

Listen to this, will you? she thought. Incredible. They had her talking like them.

The girl behind the counter at the Dairy Queen wore puce lipstick heavily outlined in brown, and she made Jimmy repeat his order three times. Marcia talked to girls like her all day (you could win them over by just admiring their earrings) and had once been that girl, but Jimmy was rattled. Marcia put her arms around Jimmy and Kaye while they waited. "Hello, three musketeers," the girl said, when she came back with their orders.

They took the ice cream—two double chocolates and one vanilla-chocolate swirl—and they each tucked into their cones with a happy concentration that Marcia decided (with some effort, and it wasn't easy) not to see as any sort of erotic pantomime. It seemed to be her job to take on innocence now, a trait she had never admired or had any use for before. And she was doing fine at it. Oh, who would have thought?

"The intrepid travelers find refreshment," Jimmy said.

What Lasts

When my sister got married, the wedding was lavish, in what my mother called a relaxed way. The bride wore beaded chiffon and a veil like a mist of dry ice, a friend's dog sat with the congregation, the best man wore a tie over a T-shirt. Afterward we all went to an old midtown nightclub whose windows overlooked an expanse of starry buildings, our own beat-up New York as a sweetly twinkling night. We stuffed ourselves on lobster sausage and white chocolate mousse. My sister Tina said, "I've done well for myself, I have to say."

The groom's business partner, the guy with the naked tie, made a toast to too much happiness. Everybody got smashed at the reception. I know this is not unusual, but my family doesn't drink much, as a rule. The youthful revelers were going at it hard, and my family got swept up in the tide. Even my mother, who can be a real wet blanket, was seen dancing some kind of frug with Uncle Dave. The groom, who was paying for all this, looked watchful and modest, as he always does. I was in a good mood myself, and I went home with Denny, the partner, just that once.

But I didn't like Mark, my sister's husband, when I first met him. I thought he was too pointedly nice, too underplayed and mannerly, too much the gentleman bandit. He'd made his living as a dope smuggler (hashish and just plain marijuana), and he'd had maybe too much practice in keeping his wits about him. He was good to Tina—she always said so, and I could see that he was—and they did terrific things together: they played tennis, they went tarpon fishing in Florida, they bought a loft as big as a lake. Tina liked that kind of thing. You might say, who wouldn't? But some don't; I sort of don't.

Still, I had stopped being against Mark by the time Tina married him. He was much less flighty than Tina, more sobered by experience. My sister Tina has worked in her life but not much; mostly she has been someone's girlfriend, a real throwback. Not a crime on her part, but it has created a division between us. I am the older sister, and sometimes it's been easier to talk to Mark.

When I got fired from my job teaching painting to bratty kids in art school, it was Mark who gave me pep talks about the cycles of fortune and how only jerks have it easy and how they laughed at Thomas Edison. (Tina, on the other hand, seemed to believe that experts had ruled correctly against me.) I was broke for a long time, and my psyche didn't do well sitting around the house. Actually Mark lent me money. Tina was very proud of this.

Mark was away a lot. That was Tina's one big complaint after they were married. She never went with him, not on those trips; only Denny went. Mark had spent almost a decade as a dealer. His drugs, such as they were, didn't have the markets they'd once had, and he was starting to talk about getting into something else. From places like Turkey, he would bring back legal items he thought about importing—kilims and copperware, even foodstuffs like pomegranate syrup and date sugar. Tina was always caught up in his ideas; she could tell me at length why there were people dying to spend their dollars on tooled leather hassocks and attar of roses. Her house looked like a Grand Bazaar.

In the end Mark went into business with our Uncle Dave, who owned a chain of ladies' hosiery shops. They were those small, sad-looking storefronts with limp stockings and dingy lace panties in the windows. Dave had maybe ten of these in different boroughs. It was Mark's own idea to enlist himself in this operation, and he had to talk a startled Dave into it. The two of them had long negotiations in delis and steakhouses. Mark bantered and reasoned and pretended to retreat, while Dave snorted in amusement and smoked his disgusting Pall Malls.

I suppose Mark did this for Tina, although one branch of the family thought he was a cad just using her to get to the great underwear fortune. In truth, Mark was facing a severe employment crisis—he didn't have much of a résumé—and he and Tina had a lot of cash flowing out. It seems unlikely she would've left him if they'd had to scale back, but Mark couldn't have known that. I don't think he could have believed that of anyone; he had his own sense of how the world worked. And Tina was talking about wanting a baby.

In his early days with Dave, Mark was known at dinners for his panty hose jokes, his riotous reports of disputes with Dave about whether girdles were still worn by anyone on the planet. By wheedling and being stubborn, Mark got the stores to carry high-style exercise wear—spandex bodysuits and some really nasty-looking thong leotards. The youth element did buy them, with enthusiasm—and Dave went around saying, "This boy is not as brainless as he looks." But no one made money hand over fist; the company wasn't structured to be that sort of enterprise. Mark was always saddened by the low profit margin, such a teeny percentage compared to the sums he'd once been used to.

He cut a different figure now, in his dark suits and his daily-grind tiredness. He looked handsome but ordinary, and he was a good sport about it. He could see that the times had shifted, and he gave himself over to the new order; he knocked himself out. What disappointed him were the mingy returns, the stingy inglorious proceeds. Who could get rich this way? Perhaps he looked again at Uncle Dave and sighed.

So during a week in midwinter, in the slowest time of year for retail, Mark got on a plane and made one more trip to Turkey. He didn't take Denny. Tina was nervous. She kept calling me to have random conversations that always ended up with questions about how it was to live alone. Did I cook my own supper, did I walk home by myself late at night? She wanted to know how I managed. She was picturing the worst and trying to reason ahead to how this might become bearable.

At the end of the week, on the afternoon of the last day, she called me from the airport when Mark's plane was late. "I don't like this," she said. She knew, the way you know these things, that his plane wasn't ever coming in with him on it. "The nice part of my life is over," she said. "I think." I asked if she wanted me to come to the airport and wait with her. "What's the point?" she said. "Thank you, but there's no point."

Two hours later she called me, all giddy and delirious. Mark was back, Mark was great. He looked very excellent. "Never, never fly Turkish Airlines," she said. "They're never on schedule, they're idiots, they're doofuses all around. Remember that."

When I stopped by the loft a few days later, Mark looked as happy as I'd ever seen him. His face was foxy and younger. You would have thought he had been to a health spa instead of running around risking his neck. I told him his tan made him radiant, not an adjective you use for a man, but he did look rosy and heroic. He kept hugging Tina, who was cheerful herself and did a lot of giggling.

What now? I thought. But already Mark was back at his same old grimy post with Dave, where he apparently meant to stay. "Dave's Cheap-o-rama," Mark called it. The phone rang a number of times while I was there, but if Mark had two jobs now, he didn't mind. He took the phone calls in the bedroom—all I could hear was an occasional laugh—and he came out breezy and cheerful, but he didn't brag around me.

Mark stayed in high spirits for months. He went to the gym every day before work; he played tennis at six in the morning. He argued merrily with Dave about push-up bras. He seemed loose and amused all the time. Invoices, inventories, billing cycles, it was all a hoot to him. This last dope run (and Tina said it had to be his last) buoyed him up for a long time.

But in the warm weather, Tina complained that just when she wanted to take off on weekends, Mark wouldn't go out of the house. Somehow he had gotten into the habit of staying in and napping all day on Saturday and Sunday. Mostly in the afternoons, but sometimes he took a snooze before lunch too. He made plans and then lost interest in them. "What are you, eighty-five years old?" Tina would say. She would sit on his lap and try to nuzzle him into activity. But neither insults nor sweetness made him budge. On weeknights he sat watching sports on TV, his feet on the hassock, his eyes straight ahead. He snapped at Tina if she talked to him. In the mornings, she found him asleep on the couch with his clothes on.

He was smoking a lot of dope, but he had always smoked a lot of dope. When I saw Mark, I said, "So do you feel crappy or what?"

"I'm laying low," Mark said. "Is there a reason I have to go do something every minute? I'm pausing and resting. I'll run around later. Your sister needs a hobby."

Mark wasn't thinner, but he did look pale and defeated; his eyes seemed unfocused and he looked done with things. Perhaps he was just sick already of being a guy in a suit; perhaps he'd begun to see what exile from his old occupation was going to mean.

I tried to get him to talk about Wimbledon, which was on TV. Good match so far? Not really. Two women were playing fierce tennis in a light summer rain, which continued long enough to stop the game. I talked Mark into playing poker then, which I believe I play better than Tina. I lost eighty dollars to him, and he was in a better mood by the time I left.

Tina, who had won six dollars from me herself, said poker was the answer, definitely. But at work that week, Mark fainted in the men's room. One of the clerks came in and found him on the floor, groaning and trying to get up, groping around on the tile. The wall behind him was streaked with blood where he had hit his head going down. He was tangled up in his pants. "This is no good, is it?" Mark said, when the clerk came in.

The doctor who bandaged Mark's head in the emergency room said the cut wasn't bad and Mark had a hard head, but he wanted to send Mark upstairs for some tests. Then Mark had to come back for more tests. "Do you know how much blood there is in the human body?" Tina said. "Only a gallon, in the average grown male. Do you know how much they've taken out already, with their little syringes?"

But it was his blood that was the trouble. They kept counting its elements and not liking how they added up. In the end what the tests found was a raging weakness among the red blood cells; they were fragile and misshapen and short-lived. What Mark had was a rare and violent kind of anemia, with no known cure. He was going to keep getting weaker, and he would have rounds of fevers and dizziness and joint pain; it was going to get hard for him to move around. The progress of the disease would be episodic and slow. Transfusions—many and often—and drugs would help him, but only for so long.

I thought about blood when I heard this. I thought of our selves as containers of bright fluid, the vascular systems like big complicated vases. What confused me was that this vital brightness could be counted, as if everything in the world were an amount. As if Mark were an amalgam of sums, a list whose figures were short.

I did not hear the news from Tina, who was too furious to speak to anyone the first few days. I heard it from our mother, who lives in Florida by herself, and who said, "I still can't believe it, because it's like something fell from the sky on his head."

Tina threw out everything in their house from Turkey. She was bitter against Turkey, where she knew Mark should never, never have gone. She wrapped every vase, every tile, every hassock, every earring, in triple bags of plastic—who knew what contagion they still had in them?—and dragged them down to the street for garbage collection, including a very valuable and heavy rug. She tossed them in a Dumpster so no bum would go through them. Mark was not home at the time and was quite upset when he found out; he had liked those objects. There was no reason to think that his illness had been caught anywhere; it had been asleep in his genes, waiting all along.

"Listen to me now. Are you listening? Was that rug *yours*?" Mark said. "No, it was *mine*." Mark ordered Tina to bring all the stuff back, and they shouted about this for a while, until Mark went out to get it himself. He climbed into the Dumpster, and he was standing on rubble from a wrecked building, torn lumber and metal cable, opening up bags of other people's kitchen garbage, while Tina yelled down to him that he was too brain damaged and too crazy to ever be normal and healthy like a regular person. In the end Mark brought back all the Turkish items, despite Tina's screaming and the fact that the stuff smelled like rotted compost by then.

I had a different view from Tina's. I thought Tina should shut up, and I said so; I am her sister. A month or so later, when I saw them at a party at Denny's, Mark was having a bad reaction to one of the drugs they were giving him. It had caused an inflammation in his joints, especially in his legs, and he was walking like someone who has to think about every step. He looked stately as a result, although this was not his goal. He sat stiff-backed in a chair next to Denny. He made fun of his friend Phil's new haircut ("What did you say to the barber about his mother?") and the music on the stereo ("Whose garage was this tape made in?"), and Denny said a few things about Mark's taste in sports jackets. I thought Mark was doing well, and it seemed to me that his years as a dope dealer—his practice in not panicking and his belief in carrying anything off with a good front—were not serving him badly. Not at all; so far.

Tina was having more trouble. She was outraged at the turn things had taken, and her mouth had a different, tight set to it. She looked particularly ferocious when she smiled. She gave me one of those terrible smiles when I came up to her at the party. "Teen," I said. "You look good."

"Why did I come to this party?" Tina said. "I can't believe I'm here."

"You can just stand here and talk to me," I said. "Nobody cares. What difference does it make?"

"I hate everyone in this room," Tina said.

"The food is good," I said.

"It's cheap," Tina said. "Cheese and bread and olives, any fool can buy them for nothing."

"Hey," I said. "Is money everything?"

"It is to Mark," Tina said.

Mark himself was crossing our path at that moment, in his newly elderly way. He was on his way to the telephone in Denny's kitchen, to call Sports-Phone for the scores. "What a fanatic," I said. I thought, this is what sports are for, to be a diversion from day-to-day woes.

"He's obsessed," Tina said. "You don't know the half of it. The week he stayed home from work I couldn't stand it."

Mark came out of the kitchen cursing to himself. "Bad news for your team?" I said.

"Bad news for his wallet," Tina said.

Mark went right past Tina without saying a word and walked back to Denny.

"It's his own fault," Tina said. "If he loses billions of dollars, it's not my fault."

Nothing was Tina's fault and that was the part that was making her wild. What had she done to bring this illness into their house? Nothing, nothing. And she had always been so hardheaded, in her lighthearted way; so practical. She had chosen what she thought would last. Solid objects, palpable pleasures. All her mercenary, gold-digging, fun-loving traits were about hoarding up, digging in, getting a good grounding. That was Tina.

"Are you fighting with Mark?" I said. "Give the man a break."

"You have always sided with him," Tina said. "You don't live with him. You don't know what living with someone is like. You have no idea."

"Why don't you just pick a fight with everyone in this room?" I said. "There are a lot of people here you could start up with."

"No, there aren't," Tina said. "Not a single person has any idea."

In a sense it was true—when I glanced around, it looked to me too like a roomful of laughing idiots. Of course they were at a party; they were acting like people at a party. One of those idiots was Mark, who had visibly recovered from his sports disappointment and was grinning away with Denny.

"Mark is cutting loose," I said. "Good for him."

Tina did soften when I said this. "He wants to go to Bali in the fall," she said. "Just to see it. It's not a bad idea, is it? He has good ideas."

Someone turned the music up very loud at this point, and a couple near us started dancing so we had to back into a corner. Denny decided that he and I had to repeat our version of the Funky Chicken that had been such a standout at the wedding. I did not feel that this could be duplicated at will, and I was more or less right, but we bopped around decently for a while. We were doing a slow number, not too sleazily, when I said, "Mark's in good spirits. Despite that killer medication they gave him. I couldn't believe he went back to work so fast."

"Well," Denny said. "You know how honorable he is. He owes old Dave a ton of money."

"Since when?" I said.

"Whoops," Denny said. "Forget that topic."

I was sorry to put Denny in a bad position, but I wormed the facts out of him anyway. Not that they were so hard to guess. I suppose I had known for a while that Mark liked to bet on the games he put in all those hours watching. This was between him and his bookie, as far as I was concerned, as long as Tina didn't complain directly. But in the weeks since the news about his illness—"the verdict from the court of doom," as Denny called it—Mark had been applying much bigger sums. Mark had gotten very ambitious.

"Why would he decide to think he was lucky now?" I said.

"That's not it," Denny said.

"What's it then?"

"Oh, you know. He had to get a taste of it. He got hungry for glory."

I thought of Mark in his radiant phase: how happy he was when his deeds were bearing fruit. I had a sudden picture of the Mark of the future, confined to the white expanse of the bedroom in their loft, intoning his bets from his pillow, like a Mafia don in prison. In my imagination he seemed methodical and debonair. Victorious.

Except that right now he was doing nothing but losing his shirt, apparently. Glory, my foot. He could pull the whole show down around them, if he wasn't careful. Then where would they be, he and Tina both? I tried to get Denny to tell me how much Mark had borrowed from Dave, but he balked on that one. "A lot? More than four digits?" I said. "More than the price of a Hyundai? More than it would cost to go to an Ivy League school for a year?" Nothing doing. Denny's lips were sealed.

Then the song was over, and some woman with a ponytail like a geyser wanted to dance the next one with Denny. I let him go, not that I had a big choice. I went to go sit near Mark, who was viewing the dancing from an imperial armchair. "Your pal Denny tired me out," I said. "The man's a demon."

"That's him," Mark said. "The devil in Reeboks."

"Look at him," I said. "He's forgotten me already. Short attention span."

"Tell me about it," Mark said. "In Turkey I used to have to remind him all the time what country he was in."

At the wedding my Aunt Belle was sure that Denny was Mark's brother, but in fact very few of Mark's relatives had been at the wedding. His mother was dead, and he had a father in Oregon he was not on good terms with. He seemed to have led most of his adult life without a family. He had us now, of course. And Denny, who was devoted but not reliable. It occurred to me that none of this was going to make the years ahead any easier for him.

Tina came over and sat down next to me on the couch. "You're drinking beer," she said to Mark.

Mark pretended to look at his bottle of Rolling Rock in astonishment. "Is that what this is?"

"He's not supposed to have that with his medication," Tina told me. "I can't stand it. I think I'm going out of my mind."

"You are, a little," Mark said.

"Goddamned right," Tina said.

"Time to cool out. Wait till we get to Bali."

"What are you going to pay for Bali with?" Tina said. "You can't even pay your stupid doctors. My sister's not going to lend you any money. She doesn't have any. So she's no help. You can go work on someone else."

Mark looked away—he was probably thinking about just walking off, except that getting out of the chair would have been a clumsy move for him then. He turned back and gave Tina a long, cutting stare. "Go home," he said.

"*What?*" Tina said. "What did you say?"

"Excuse me," I said. "You don't need me for this discussion."

I went over to the drinks table and stood around by myself for a long time. All of a sudden I wanted to go home myself—none of us belonged here—although Tina, especially, had been a great partier not so long ago. Almost everything about Tina had changed since the advent of Mark's illness. She had never been mean-tempered before—willful, yes, a princess of caprice at times—but not harsh and snappish.

Mark, on the other hand, was much the same. That was Tina's complaint. That was the part she couldn't stand. She believed he was not adapting to the crisis at hand. All her fluffy pleasantness was gone, all her professional sexy pertness. Mark, on his side, claimed to feel gypped and misled. Who was this person hectoring him with herbal teas and root concoctions (she was reading a lot about natural cures), with bullying advice and prohibitions? Nurse Ratched, Mark said, Miss Beulah the Prison Matron.

Tina found me awhile later, standing in the same place by the drinks. "I have to ask you," she said, "can I stay over at your house tonight? I might want to stay at your place for a while. Is that all right?"

Tina had been crying—her face was raw and puffy—but I had no pity and I had a very low opinion of her right then. "How is Mark going to manage?" I said.

"Better without me," she said. "Better without showing off for me."

"Tina. It's not just for you that he does it."

"Forget it," Tina said. "I'll find someone else to stay with."

And she did. Ten minutes later I saw her leave with Francie Nickerson, an ex-neighbor from her old building. When Mark came near me, I was so embarrassed for Tina I could just about speak. "What a jerk," I said.

"We had words," Mark told me. "I said a few heavy things myself."

I thought he sounded like a pop tune, but why should he delve deep to give me a report? Let him use that smooth voice, I didn't care.

I went to confer with Denny. Shouldn't he try to talk Mark into staying over at his house tonight? I thought that if Mark needed, for instance, help getting out of bed in the morning, Denny would be the one to do it. Denny, who was all sweaty and wet-headed from dancing, looked surprised at the whole idea. "Sure, if he wants," Denny said. "Don't worry."

I was worrying over my tequila when Mark came over to me. He said, "I'll see you home in a cab if you want to go now."

So I went out with him. He did fine on the stairs, rocking his way down slowly. I hovered, but he didn't lean on me. "Tina is acting so out of line now," I said. "What is the matter with her brain?"

Mark shrugged. My comments were not that interesting to him. "It's not a big deal," he said.

AND TINA DID COME BACK the next day; I heard later that she turned up for breakfast with a bag of bagels. So it was not a big deal, her tantrum of the night. As Mark had known. Or he might have meant that none of the petty upheavals of life seemed very important to him just then. That's what I thought at the time.

Probably Mark and Tina had one of those blissful, lusty reunions people have after fights. Certainly they seemed to have reached a more-or-less permanent truce by the time I saw them. Neither of them was speaking confidentially to me. I'd gotten caught in the crunch, someone they both thought of as disloyal.

After their feuding, one of the compromises they apparently reached at this time was to go for weekends to the beach, a wholesome excursion that took them out of the house. On Fridays, Tina drove them out to Montauk, where they stayed at a particularly nice inn and came back with golden tans. If Mark listened to baseball games on the radio while they lay out on the sand, at least this listening was folded into a leisurely summer day.

I saw them for dinner a few times. Tina liked to eat outside, and in the humid city nights we would sit out at spindly tables on the sidewalk. Tina, who is blonde, was so tanned she looked like a photo negative, and Mark, who is dark to begin with, glowed in his white shirts. "God, you look pale," Mark said to me. "What are you, sick?" Mark's walk was much better since they had changed his drugs, and it was hard not to think he really was healthy and had more of a chance than we'd been told. We get told things all the time that turn out to be dead wrong.

Mark paid for me too at those dinners; he always acted like an older relative to me, although I am five months older than he is. With Tina he was like an indulgent uncle, amused at her whims. She was perky again, girlish and lively. I thought Mark had won some sort of battle about what he didn't want changed. He had his beliefs, such as they were. Mark was very much at his ease those nights.

It made me serene that summer to see them. A sunny influence from their warm-weather spirits settled over me, and when a man I had just met asked me if I wanted to go to Wyoming for a month with him, I thought, why not? How many lives am I going to get? He was a quiet, untalkative person, but full of bold suggestions like this one; it was the combination that got me so attracted. And it turned out I liked Wyoming. In the daytime I worked on paintings in the shed, while Gene, my friend, went around taking photographs, which was what he was there to do. The mountains were around us on all sides, steep and cloudy in the distance. I didn't exactly know what to do with them—I had not been outside the city much before—but from my window in the shed I watched them, the blunt shapes with their backdrop of sky. At night it was chilly, and we sat around the fireplace. The house we were using was something between a cabin and a shack, and it smelled of woodsmoke all the time.

It smelled also of incense. Twice a day Gene chanted a Buddhist sutra and lit incense sticks; he did this very matter-of-factly and would have gone off to a separate room had there been one. As it was, the heavy muskiness reminded me of hashish, and also of the patchouli we once used to burn to cover its scent. I thought of Mark, of course—Mr. Smoke—and once in the night the phrase *ashes to ashes* made me gasp from sadness. I lay awake in dread and sadness.

And I was afraid then that in the morning I wasn't going to be able to stand being around that smoky reek all the time, but by day the ceremonial wisps of smoke seemed what they were supposed to be, matter exhaling itself into odor, burnt resin passing into pure air.

When I came back to New York in the fall, almost everything about the city was loud and stylized to me. Gene and I went around saying, What is this rush rush rush? Who are these crazy maniac New Yorkers? Still it was my home. I had gotten into several quarrels with Gene on the car ride back, and I couldn't tell how serious they were and I wanted to call Tina right away to ask her opinion. I had talked to her once from Wyoming, and she had said things were good, Mark was doing really well.

When I called, it was Mark who answered the phone. This was in the middle of the afternoon on a weekday, and I thought at first that it must be one of the Jewish holidays creeping up early this year. "I took my own holiday," Mark said. "I quit the business."

"You did what?" I sounded rude, but I was thinking about his employability and his health insurance.

"We had a difference of opinion," Mark said. "Your Uncle Dave let me down when I needed a favor. I just have always been the sort of person who doesn't appreciate it when people do not have any loyalty and they go around saying I'm draining them dry."

Mark had asked for another loan, it seemed, and Dave had turned his back on him. *Dave*, that inept trafficker in outdated corsets and prissy anklets, had declined to stand behind *Mark*. Mark could not get over the betrayal. It seemed to embitter him far more than his illness did. He would raise the money some other way, but he couldn't ever trust Dave again.

I hadn't heard Mark in this particular style of outrage before, and it jolted me. I wondered how Tina was taking this. Not well, probably. Mark said she had stepped out after breakfast, and he didn't know where she was. Probably she would be back soon. Did I want to leave a message?

I tried Denny right away, to see what else he could tell me. "Welcome home to the money capital of the world," Denny said. "Mark has been out there acting like some sort of high-flying financial hysteric." Mark had had the idea that if he could get a lot of cash together, he could do a number of things: he could go to Bali and lull out and watch sunsets on the beach; he could go to Mexico, where some quack dispensed a regimen of root powders that Tina believed would help him; he could get sicker and start to die and know there was enough of a cache left behind to cover Tina for a while. How Mark thought he could do all this by guessing right about the point spread on games was a big mystery to Denny too.

Since I was so attached to Mark, the dogged nerviness in all of this struck me first, Mark trying to flash his cash at the Grim Reaper. But now he had really made a mess. What was going to happen? Denny said, "There are individuals in the world who make loans." This was not soothing information. "Don't worry," Denny said. To Denny, too, money was a mercurial substance.

"The bad thing," Denny said, "the one bad thing, would be if Tina left him."

"He has friends," I said. "He has you. I'm here too."

Denny ignored this. Perhaps he thought Mark was passing the point where friends were much good to him. What about Tina? he wanted to know. She wouldn't leave really? I said I wasn't sure, and there was a silence over the phone, a long helpless pause.

IT WAS MANY DAYS before I had any word from Tina, no matter how many messages I left. Mark wasn't answering the phone either. "Maybe they went away?" Gene said. They had gone somewhere, as it turned out, on their own journey right within the four walls of their loft. Mark had a bad bout with his illness; pains in his stomach made him double up, and his hands and feet swelled horribly. In the crisis Tina ministered to him quite tenderly—she can be gracious and funny, the best kind of nurse. All of this had, of course, bound her more firmly to Mark and given her a new angelic identity and a clearer path.

Mark told everyone later that she fed him gruel, actually grains and soups sent from the health food store. Tina wouldn't go outside herself for two weeks straight; she wouldn't leave when she saw what she had, Mark in bed, jackknifed with pain. Mark too sick to get up by himself. My sister is a practical person.

By the time she was willing to talk to me, she had been quite busy. On her own, the crisply devoted wife with an ailing spouse, she had gone to a bank and gotten an equity loan on their loft—for all his new careerism on this side of the law, Mark was afraid of banks—and she had used this to cover Mark's current debts, with the remainder almost enough to pay off the old loan from Dave. This made Dave a lot mellower. He was ready to talk reasonably about buying out Mark's share in the business in installments. But by this time Mark was feeling much better again and decided he might as well go back to work. "Back to the salt mines," Dave said. But he was quite tickled, and the two of them celebrated Mark's first day back at the office by going off to the steakhouse they always liked and getting potted on vodka gimlets, which Mark was not supposed to do.

"We're out of the woods," Tina said. This was so clearly untrue that I didn't say anything to deny it.

Tina was ready to rest, and who could blame her? She felt that she had passed through something—or, rather, she and Mark had passed through it together—and she was ready to be contented again. She spoke Mark's name with such sweetness that I did call up Denny and tell him not to worry.

She talked about Mark constantly. And she was glad to offer me useless advice about Gene. "Time will tell," she said, and also, "Wait and see." "Be patient," she suggested, from the magisterial standpoint of her abiding matrimony. "Tina," I said, "forget I asked." But she was resting; she had become the matron of restful views.

When Tina is happy she spends money, and so she'd gone out and gotten things for the house, including a small and beautiful Turkish rug, an old one that Mark said she paid too much for. But he was enormously pleased with it; it seemed to be a sign of something understood by them together. They walked around it with care, they looked down into it as if it were a pond. Its main color was a deep red, with black and yellow designs. Mark was still moving stiffly, when I visited them, and Tina occasionally took his elbow. Later I tried to tell Gene about the two of them, in the sleek whiteness of their loft, circling that rug.

Through most of this time, Gene and I were going strong, definitely a live item. "The physical is so important," Tina said to me on the phone. It took me a moment to realize she meant sex. I was thinking about health. But Tina was busy cackling away about how Gene sounded like someone who knew what went where in bed. "Tina," I said. I was going to make a joke about how a married person like herself probably could hardly remember these things, but I thought better of it, not knowing now what their life was like that way.

Whatever it was like, Tina had settled herself into it. She showed a kind of bridal interest in the house. In the glassy expanse of that loft, all the copperware trays and Turkish tiles were out again, in careful display. In fact there seemed to be more of them, a refreshed collection.

When I brought Gene to their house for dinner, I thought how well-nested they seemed. They fed us a very delicious meal, little hens they barbecued out on the fire escape. Mark and Tina looked like a particularly stylish suburban couple, in their butcher aprons, out there with the dark smoke wafting up to the next floors. "It's illegal to do this," Mark said. "No wonder I like it."

Gene and I sat watching the last pink tinge of a gorgeous chemical sunset. When the sky turned twilight blue, the food was ready. Mark tried to get me to bet on which bird was cooked the rarest. "Just kidding," he said.

"How could she tell in this light?" Tina said. "I can just about see my own fork." But they kept the lamps unlit. The plates seemed to be floating on the glass table. A moth flew into the salad, and Tina got to say, "How much can it eat?" Mark sat listening. He was attentive but dreamy, like someone staring out at water, or like one of those men sitting around a Greek village at dusk.

He was actually looking younger, although the boyish freckles that had appeared recently were from iron deposits in the skin and not from the sun. I had to keep from touching my own face when I looked at him.

Gene had his arm on the back of my chair, between courses, and Tina smiled benignly at us, the new twosome. "Maybe we'll go to Wyoming next summer," she said.

"Is it hot there?" Mark said. "It's not hot?"

"It's great," Gene said.

"Know how I used to scare Tina when she was little?" I said. "I made her think that if she stayed in the sun too long she could ignite all of a sudden, like a piece of paper on a mirror."

"No," Mark said. "Who would believe that?"

"I think I believed it," Tina said. "I think I remember."

But it was one of those stories that couldn't ever be convincing; it was too improbable when told to a bunch of people sitting around a table at night in their adult bodies, these bodies that we will all pass out of.

THE AUTHOR

Shari Caroline Diamond

Joan Silber is the author of the novels *Household Words*, which won the PEN/Hemingway Award, and *In the City* (both published by Viking Penguin). Her short fiction has appeared in *The New Yorker*, *Ploughshares*, *The Voice Literary Supplement*, *The Paris Review*, and other magazines. She has received grants from the Guggenheim Foundation, the NEA, and the New York Foundation for the Arts. She lives in New York City.